Alan Hunter was born in Hoveton, Norfolk in 1922. He left school at the age of fourteen to work on his father's farm, spending his spare time sailing on the Norfolk Broads and writing nature notes for the *Eastern Evening News*. He also wrote poetry, some of which was published while he was in the RAF during the Second World War. By 1950, he was running his own bookshop in Norwich. In 1955, the first of what would become a series of forty-six George Gently novels was published. He died in 2005, aged eighty-two.

The Inspector George Gently series

Gently Does It
Gently by the Shore
Gently Down the Stream
Landed Gently
Gently Through the Mill
Gently in the Sun
Gently with the Painters
Gently to the Summit
Gently Go Man
Gently Where the Roads Go
Gently Floating
Gently Sahib

Gently Sahib

Alan Hunter

ROBINSON

Constable & Robinson Ltd
55–56 Russell Square
London WC1B 4HP
www.constablerobinson.com

First published by Cassell & Co. Ltd., London, 1964

This edition published by Robinson,
an imprint of Constable & Robinson Ltd., 2012

A copy of the British Library Cataloguing in
Publication data is available from the British Library

ISBN 978-1-78033-154-6 (paperback)
ISBN 978-1-78033-155-3 (ebook)

Typeset by TW Typesetting, Plymouth, Devon

Printed and bound by CPI Group (UK) Ltd, Croydon, CR0 4YY

3 5 7 9 10 8 6 4 2

HELEN ADELAIDE ISABELLA
*who must wait a long time
before she can read this
book*

*The characters and events in this book are fictitious;
the locale is sketched from life.*

CHAPTER ONE

POLICEMAN SHOOTS TIGER
Country Town Terrorized
Attack On Butcher's Van

I T WAS A small town.

Driving through it, you were annoyed by its complex of streets. At the same time you were impressed by an old-world spaciousness, a clumsy charm.

You drove downhill through the suburb streets then uphill again to the town centre. So you saw a citadel of plastered gable-ends and rusty brick among many dark trees.

That looked peaceful, had repose. Yet actually it was a busy market town.

It contained any number of old-established businesses and had a bustling market on Wednesdays and Saturdays.

There was money in the town, well-to-do people. All around it lay rich farmlands. It was handy for

1

London, though not too close, and you could drive in easily for a day's shopping or a show.

Also the place had social 'tone', for there were two great estates within a few miles of it. Bordering its river stood the remains of a huge abbey and beside the abbey a modest cathedral church.

Yet the 'tone' was affable, easy-going, like the old houses with their big doors and bow windows.

Life was busy, but had poise.

This was Abbotsham (pop. 19,023).

For six hours yesterday morning panic reigned in placid Abbotsham. A hungry Bengal tiger roamed the deserted streets. Escaping from the farm of Hugh Groton, an animal importer, it made its way into the sleeping town. A 76-year-old pensioner, Mrs Annie Short, was first to give the alarm.

Annie Short had a daughter living in a village seven miles off. To this village Annie could sometimes get a lift on a fruit-pickers' bus. The bus left the station yard at six thirty a.m. The old lady was a dairyman's widow and so was used to early rising.

At five a.m. she rose and washed and put on her best black dress. All was quiet. From across the road she could hear the gentle wheeze of the gasworks.

Her cottage was one of a row in Gas Lane, which was a cul-de-sac off Nelson Street and which had at the end of it a fellmonger's warehouse which smelled badly in warm weather.

It was warm weather now. She sniffed a little while getting her breakfast.

At six ten a.m. she unbolted her street door.

She saw the tiger standing just outside.

Annie Short, who had handled bulls, didn't scream or faint; instead she seized the walking stick which stood by the door and thrust it sharply at the tiger's eyes.

The tiger leaped backwards and showed its teeth in a thundering snarl. It crouched. It stared at Annie and her stick, its empty yellow eyes smouldering.

'Shoo!' Annie said. 'Shoo! Go away, you bad boy.'

Then she calmly bolted the door again and went out at the back to waken her neighbour.

Her neighbour, Mrs Onley, had a phone which her children had installed. Annie Short rang the police and informed them of the tiger.

'There's one of them zoo creatures gallivanting in the lane. Hadn't you better come along and see to it, together?'

'There's a what, missus?'

'A big old tiger thing. I don't know what you'd call it.'

'A tiger?'

'Ah. Something of that sort. Do you send a man round after him.'

The desk sergeant held his hand over the phone.

'Timmo! Here's a job for you. Lady reports a tiger in Gas Lane. You keep rabbits at home, don't you?'

Then to the telephone he said: 'Right you are, missus, I'm sending a lion tamer.'

'So I should think,' Annie Short said.

But when Timmo arrived, the tiger had gone.

Savage with hunger, the great beast attacked a butcher's van driven by Mr Harry Birdbrook. While it was devouring his meat Mr Birdbrook succeeded in climbing a wall.

Mr Birdbrook also set out early that morning. He had a flourishing round in the nearby villages few of which had butchers shops.

In addition to orders which had been phoned in he carried a supply of dressed meat which, laid out in dishes under a white cloth, was intended to attract casual custom. To make the display effective he had an open-sided van. He drove the van sedately, rarely exceeding thirty miles an hour.

Mr Birdbrook was a massive man and he regarded himself as his best advertisement. He had rolling cheeks that resembled those of the model piglets in his shop window.

When he left the shop in the Buttermarket he drove down Friargate into Station Road.

It was six twenty a.m. by the station clock and fruit-pickers were collecting near a works bus.

Suddenly they scattered, as though Mr Birdbrook were a terrible apparition; he blinked his round eyes at them in amazement. Could they be having him on, or something?

Tilting his nose, he drove past the station and took a side road that led to Firstfield, a narrow road between high hedges which it was time somebody cut. Here he had another surprise. He met a postman cycling towards him.

Almost at once the postman dismounted, or rather fell off his bike, and dived into the hedge.

What was it about? A sudden call of nature? Or were they all in league to make a fool of him?

He frowned as he passed the thrown-down bike, one wheel of which was still spinning.

A hundred yards farther on the road turned sharply to the right and it was here, in his offside mirror, that Mr Birdbrook caught sight of the tiger. He gave a yelp and bounced in his seat and sent the van swerving across the road.

Impossible! Yet it was there, intently loping along behind him.

A tiger at least as big as a carthorse – big enough to swallow him in a couple of gulps!

Mr Birdbrook stabbed at the accelerator. The van picked up to a steady forty. This was its maximum, for it was an old van, but it didn't seem to discommode the tiger.

Worse, it blew the cloths off the meat, exposing some prime steak and a dish of sausages.

Raising dust, the tiger put on speed. Now it was bounding along level with the van.

Then it sprang. It crashed down into the van with a weight that nearly turned it over. Both the back springs were broken at once and the offside tyre was fouled and blew. Mr Birdbrook bawled, the van swerved over the verge, struck the hedge, heeled, and stopped.

Mr Birdbrook, uninjured, burst out of the cab in a tumult of flailing limbs.

Across the road was a boundary wall which enclosed a plantation belonging to Teyn Lodge. It was a six-foot wall, and in the normal way beyond Mr Birdbrook's powers to scale.

Now he crossed the road and skipped up the wall in a single convulsive effort, then clawed into the branches of a big oak tree that swept the wall at that point.

Could a tiger climb a tree? He had a horrid idea he'd read it could.

But he was stuck; his bough was isolated. He could only cling to it, his eyes bulging like gooseberries.

Meanwhile the tiger, having made its kill, was settling down to gnaw and tear at the meat. It liked the sausages, drawing out strings of them and severing mouthfuls with a toss of its head.

But when it had finished these hors d'oeuvres?

Mr Birdbrook closed his eyes.

The only sounds were of birds singing and the fearsome tearing noises made by the tiger.

Minutes passed. Then the tearing noises were interrupted by a whimpering snarl.

Mr Birdbrook closed his eyes tighter, began to mumble some prayers he remembered.

Another snarl, then the frightful sound of the tiger jumping down from the van; but also a different sound, a sharp scolding, challenging yelp.

Mr Birdbrook opened an eye.

What he saw he could scarcely credit.

Not twenty yards from the crouched tiger stood Suki, the Teyn Lodge Pekinese.

The Pekinese had its head held back, its button eyes staring indignantly at the tiger, and the latter, flat down and ready to spring, was waving its tail and showing huge yellow teeth.

The Pekinese yelped again. It began stalking towards the tiger. It was about the size of one of the tiger's forepaws and it strutted without haste on its bow legs.

The tiger gave a whining snarl and shuffled itself backwards a few feet.

The Peke came on.

The tiger retreated farther.

The Peke set up a furious barking.

In a flash, its nerve breaking, the tiger leaped up and began to run.

The Peke, in an ecstasy of indignant barking, shot down the road in pursuit, breaking off only when the tiger, with tail trailing, galloped panic-stricken round the bend.

Then the Peke trotted back again, grumbling and yelping, and stopped to look at Mr Birdbrook.

Mr Birdbrook also looked at the Peke. Though he had probably forgotten it when he talked to the reporters.

Police armed with rifles patrolled a wide area around Firstfield Road. Later the military were called in and a contingent of the RAF Regiment. Nothing was seen of the desperate animal for several hours after the attack on the van.

The trouble was, from the police point of view, that nobody would take the tiger seriously.

Loudspeaker vans were sent round the town

warning people to keep off the streets, but that only seemed to bring them out, including the children, who were greatly excited.

Also, it was the Saturday market, which brought in crowds of country people; even if they had wanted to keep off the streets they had nowhere to go except the pubs and shops.

As for the market, it continued as usual. It would take more than a tiger to stop that. The big square of stalls, with lights blazing under striped canopies, was crowded with shoppers from breakfast-time onwards.

The market was entertainment. Cheap-jacks thronged one side of it. Stolid-faced country folk grouped silently round them to be harangued in Cockney and Brummagem accents. Plates were slammed together to show their soundness, rolls of printed cotton went flapping down counters.

One man, styled The Glassware King, smashed a tumbler and ate it at the start of his performance.

And nobody really believed in the tiger – hadn't it escaped to the fields, anyway?

In the Abbey Gardens children, tired of waiting to see it, improvised a game called 'Tiger, Tiger'.

And the policemen too felt a little silly, strolling about the streets with rifles from the barracks. Some carried them shouldered, like sentries, some wore them slung, thumb-under-strap.

Groton, the animal dealer who owned the tiger, was cruising about in the back of a police car. He was a huge man in a khaki shirt and jodhpurs and he wore an impressive revolver in a polished leather holster.

'Don't shoot unless you have to,' he'd told the police. 'I can handle him – that's my job. I paid seven hundred and fifty for that tigger. I've some doped gee-gee waiting in the truck.'

The truck, slightly resembling a Black Maria, was an object of interest on the Abbey Plain car park. Small boys pointed out the little barred windows and fingered the scratches on the two heavy doors.

But only Groton was showing a real concern. Danger seemed so remote from the Saturday market, the busy pavements. If there was in fact a tiger – one remembered the cheetah scare at Blackheath – wouldn't someone appear with a whip and usher it back to its cage?

Meanwhile there was the shopping to do, shoes for the kids, the old man's tobacco.

And hour by hour was safely tolled by the clock on the Jew's House, a resonant chimer.

Then the famished brute appeared again, this time in the crowded Market Place. The police believe it had been lying up in a small yard behind a fish shop. Panic swept through the crowds. They rushed screaming into adjoining streets. A policeman fired at the tiger which darted into cover.

Police Constable Kennet was the man who fired at the tiger. Except for the tiger he would have been playing cricket on the village green at Cockgrave. He was a lean, strong-boned man, a fast bowler and a middling bat. He was patrolling the east side of the

Market Place while Police Constable Bulley patrolled the west side.

The tiger appeared opportunely, when Police Constable Kennet had come to the south end of his beat.

A moment before he'd watched Police Constable Bulley slip into the convenience by the Jew's House.

The tiger emerged with composure. It stood blinking its eyes at the top of an alley. For several moments it went unnoticed and remained peering at the stalls and lazily stretching.

Then it yawned – and one of the cheap-jacks found himself peering into a vast throat.

He gave a wavering sort of yell and overbalanced from the box on which he had been demonstrating butane lighters.

In doing so he upset a case of lighters, which went shimmying around on the flagstones, and made such a commotion that all attention was temporarily centred on himself.

Then he got up and began running and shouting:

'Get out of here – it's that blinking tiger!'

And there were screams and other shouts and a sudden rushing and violent scramble.

Yet strangely enough, not everybody ran. Quite half the crowd, after the first scatter, came to a stand again at a little distance. Some were climbing on stalls, others catching up impromptu weapons. It was those at the back who caught the panic and dashed into shops and into side streets.

Only Police Constable Kennet stood his ground, but behind him a semicircle formed.

He could feel them there, tense, watching him, the man who must do something about the tiger.

And the tiger blinked at this sudden confusion and gave a feeble flick of his tail. Then he made to yawn again, thought better of it, dropped his head and prepared to slink off.

'Use your gun!' someone shouted. 'There's women and kids back here, mate.'

'Shoot the bleeder – don't be a mug.'

'Shoot him while you have the chance!'

Police Constable Kennet unslung his rifle. He didn't want to shoot the tiger. His instinct told him that just then the tiger was comparatively undangerous.

But after all, it was a tiger . . . and women were screaming there, behind him.

He threw the rifle to his shoulder, fired, missed the tiger by yards.

And the tiger, snarling, bounded away to vanish through the doorway of the convenience.

Police Constable Bulley, who saw service with the Sufolks during the war, was searching the premises when the tiger entered. 'It was a terrible moment,' he told our reporter. 'Luckily I had remembered the old army drill – one up at the spout. He got it straight through the heart.'

In fact, Police Constable Bulley had his back to the doorway at the critical moment of the tiger's entry. He had stood his rifle down inside, since it tended to slip off his shoulder. He was preoccupied; he heard Police Constable Kennet's shot without appreciating its import.

A moment later there was chaos. He didn't have time to feel afraid.

The tiled cloister of the convenience exploded with sound that deafened him for minutes.

Along with the roar came a gasping snarl and the lumping thud of a huge body and the scraping sound of claws on tiles, then just the singing deafness in his ears.

He came about unsteadily.

The tiger was lying by the washbasin, one paw fanning weakly.

Three yards from it lay his rifle with a trickle of smoke rising from the muzzle.

The tiger was dead. It lay on its back with a pool of blood growing round it. As Police Constable Bulley stared at the tiger its paw stopped fanning, quivered, went still.

Police Constable Bulley breathed heavily. He went doubtfully to the rifle and picked it up. That's damned light on the trigger, was all he could think: they should strip that gun in the armoury.

He hefted it under his arm, got over the tiger, came sheepishly out of the convenience. Outside Police Constable Kennet stood gaping. If he was saying anything, Bulley couldn't hear him.

So ended the terror that stalked the streets of peaceful Abbotsham. Police Constable Bulley is to be recommended for a Police Medal.

Inspector Perkins, who arrived a minute later, noticed that Bulley was improperly dressed, but since he couldn't tell him without shouting he simply hurried him into the police car.

And that was all, for the moment, about the Abbotsham Tiger.

CHAPTER TWO

'THE AC WANTS to see you, sir.'

Ferrow was the second person to give him the message. Earlier, as Gently had come in from parking his car, the desk sergeant had interrupted a phone call to tell him.

'What about?' Gently had grunted.

'Don't know, sir,' the sergeant'd said.

Now, in response to the same question, Ferrow gave the same answer.

Gently stared at him grumpily before stumping upstairs to his office. So the AC wanted him, did he! Had he forgotten about Gently's leave?

Because he studied the papers over breakfast and was expert at sifting news stories, Gently was reasonably certain nothing big had come up. There'd been a bank job at Croydon, which was none of his business; a stabbing at Manchester, who wouldn't call London; and a suspected poisoning at Slough.

Was it the poisoning they were going to stick on him, probably a lengthy routine chore? If it was . . . !

He growled to himself, aimed a kick at the door of the outer office.

Inside sat Inspector Dutt, typing a report with two fingers. He grinned moonishly at his superior and stopped typing to say:

'The AC—'

'I know!' Gently snapped. 'Next thing he'll give it to the papers. What's it about?'

'About a tiger, chief.'

'About a what?'

'About a tiger.'

Gently closed the door of the outer office and leaned against it massively. He took out his pipe and struck a light for it, jetted smoke towards the ceiling.

'Dutt,' he said. 'Is this the silly season?'

'Yes, chief. Bang in the middle of it.'

'And he wants to see me about a tiger?'

'About a man about a tiger, he said, chief.'

'Just that and nothing else?'

'He said it would be right up your street. He sounded a bit tickled about it, said you wouldn't want to miss it.'

'How nice of him,' Gently said. 'Only this isn't my day for tigers.' He puffed. 'It wouldn't be a leg-pull, Dutt?'

'Don't know, chief.'

'It isn't my day for them either.''

But the Assistant Commissioner was rather vain about his sense of humour. In his student days he'd been one of a band who'd dug a hole in Oxford Circus. Nobody had interfered for three days, when the traffic was jammed as far as Holborn, and five separate authorities were exchanging bitter memos.

And now he'd been paging Gently ever since Gently set foot in the place . . .

'What's that report you've got there?'

'This? The Blazey case, chief.'

'Hurry it up and I'll take it to him. Then we'll see what it is with the tiger.'

He swept through into his office, scowled at it, tossed his hat at the peg. Apart from a return sheet his in tray was as empty as it ought to be just now.

For the next forty-eight hours he'd be available for conferences, routine, perhaps a fill-in job; but unless the heavens opened they shouldn't wrap a major case round his neck. And the heavens hadn't opened, or he'd have smelt it out in the papers. This was a leg-pull . . . another sample of the AC's dubious humour.

The phone went.

'Gently.'

'Ah, Gently. Did you get my message?'

He couldn't wait, even, till Gently condescended to appear!

'Dutt's getting out his Blazey report. I thought I'd bring it with me.'

'Never mind the Blazey case, that's finished. I want you along here directly.

'Gently – are you there?'

'Mmn,' Gently said. 'I'm here.'

'I'll expect you right away then, OK? Drop everything.'

Gently laid the phone fastidiously in its cradle again. He whistled a tune. From the outer office came the tortuous chatter of Dutt's typing. Gently rose, went to watch Dutt, who frowned as he felt Gently watching him.

'Just signing off now, sir,' Dutt said. 'Won't be another minute.'

Gently shrugged and walked over to the window.

He began to think of his fishing plans.

The Assistant Commissioner raised his glasses.

'So glad you could make it,' he said. 'I've been looking round for your resignation. But perhaps you forgot to hand it in.'

He was a thin man with a saintly expression but when he was sarcastic he was angry. Gently placed Dutt's report on the desk, remained standing and poker-faced.

'The Public Prosecutor's office—'

'Damn the Public Prosecutor's office.'

'The case is being tried on Monday.'

'I should be aware of that, Gently.'

They looked at each other. Without shifting his gaze the AC took out his handkerchief and began polishing his glasses. He was one of the very few men who could stare at Gently on even terms.

At last he said: 'Well?'

Gently cleared his throat. 'I'm not an expert . . .'

'What do you mean – not an expert?'

'I don't know anything about tigers.'

'Aha,' the AC said. 'So that's it.'

'I couldn't talk about them,' Gently said. 'Not to a man, about a tiger. Even dogs I'm not well up on.'

17

The AC went on polishing his glasses. Then he put them on with a dainty flourish.

'All right,' he said, 'I'm with you now. Message understood. You can sit down.'

'Catching tench, now—'

'Gently, sit down.'

'But I'm not an expert on tigers.'

'Sit down, man! The joke's on me.'

'I thought I should warn you,' Gently said, sitting.

The AC stared at him again, but now he was grinning. He wagged his head archly at Gently. Gently's face was still blank.

'So you thought I was having you on! Well, it may have sounded a bit like that. But I'm not, Gently. This is quite serious. We have a murder case with a tiger in it.'

'Who's the chummie?' Gently said. 'The tiger?'

'Please! I told you this was serious. But the tiger may have been used as a murder weapon, which is unique in my experience.'

The AC leaned elbows on the desk. He believed in himself as a raconteur. The wiping of the glasses, the pose with the elbows, they were all part of his act.

But he couldn't talk away the fact that Gently was on leave within forty-eight hours . . .

'You remember what happened at Abbotsham last year? Almost exactly a year today! A tiger got loose on the Friday night and was roaming the streets the next morning.

'It was a real tiger too, not just a scare somebody started. A big male, around ten feet long, which a

18

johnny had imported from Pakistan. It was a mystery how it got out. The owner was in town that night. When his two hands showed up in the morning they found the cage unbolted and the gate part open.

'The owner hared back to help the police catch it, but they didn't take it alive. When it popped up in the provision market they had to shoot it, of course.

'As far as they knew it had done no damage, other than wrecking a butcher's van. The theory was that some bright kid had let it out for a dare.'

The AC licked his lips.

'Till yesterday,' he said. 'Then something interesting turned up in the garden of a bungalow near Abbot-sham.'

Gently tapped the desk with a blunt forefinger.

'There was nothing about this in the papers.'

'Nothing, I agree. But you wait. They'll be screaming their heads off tomorrow.'

'Meanwhile . . .'

'You listen to me. This is your sort of a case. It's got everything, and we can't spoil it by sending down a nonentity.'

Gently grunted. All right – but flattery wasn't going to do it either!

'That bungalow had been empty,' the AC went on, 'since the night of the tiger. It stands a mile outside the town on the Stowmundham road. First the milkman found nobody was taking in the milk, but the owner of the bungalow was sometimes away, so the milkman just stopped delivering.

'The same thing happened with the paper boy and

the other tradesmen – they called for a while, then gave it up as a bad job. But the postman kept calling – there was always the odd circular – and at last he became curious and peeped through the letter box. What he saw was sufficiently striking for him to mention it to a bobby, and the bobby reported it to the CID, and the CID forced the door.

'Guess what they discovered.'

'A summons for the rates,' Gently said.

'All right – have your fun! They may have found soap-powder coupons too. But they also found the hall wrecked and the walls and floor spattered with blood, and a rug on the floor so impregnated with blood that you could pick it up like a sheet of hardboard. The hallstand and two chairs were smashed and an inner door hung from one hinge. And on door, walls and floor were the scars of claws – huge claws. The marks were a handspan across.

'Now laugh that off if you can.'

He paused, eyes gleaming, waiting to get his reaction. Most of the TV politicians could have taken points from the AC.

But Gently didn't react, he simply stared back, deadpanned.

'The body,' the AC said, 'was in the garden.'

'Yes,' Gently said. 'So I assumed.'

'It was a man. He was terribly mauled. They think he was aged about fifty.'

'The owner of the bungalow?'

'As far as they know. They dug him out of a flower bed. They sent in his dabs but he doesn't have form –

though oddly enough, we know of him. And right away there's a motive. His name is Shimpling. He was a blackmailer. He was our witness in the Cheyne-Chevington case – doctor who sold drugs to prostitutes.'

Gently nodded. 'That wasn't a conviction.'

'No, but Cheyne-Chevington was struck off – which you might consider as a motive for setting a tiger on Shimpling. Anyway, Shimpling owned the bungalow. He lived there under his own name. And all the collateral evidence points to him being the man they dug up.

'For example, his personal gear is still in the bungalow – clothes, medical card, a passport. There are two suitcases with his initials and a silver brush set engraved with monograms.

'They seem to have caught him on the hop. Some milk had boiled over in the kitchen. They appear to have searched the bungalow, but nobody knows if they took anything. It could be he was holding incriminating evidence which they daren't leave behind.

'Two other things, and that's the picture. First, his car is missing from the garage. Second, witnesses talk of a Mrs Shimpling, though there's no woman's gear in the bungalow. But at the time of the Cheyne-Chevington affair Shimpling had a blonde living with him – Shirley Banks, she's a prostitute. She was also a Crown witness.

'A tiger, a blonde and a body in the garden. What more do you need to get your name in the Sundays?'

Gently shrugged politely. What more indeed?

21

The AC unlatched his glasses again, beamed affectionately at Gently.

'Of course, I know you're due for leave, and I wouldn't dream of upsetting it. But you do see, don't you, that the case calls for a personality. The Press'll be there in droves, we daren't send one of the faceless brigade. So I'm asking you, for the sake of the public image, to go down there and open the batting.

'Just two days. After that we can put in a nightwatchman – and you can get on with your holiday.

'A fishing trip in Wales, isn't it?'

He leaned back, watching Gently, making the glasses swing hypnotically. In his department, he was fond of boasting, it was all done by kindness . . .

Gently sighed very quietly. 'So what's his name?' he asked.

'Whose name?'

'The animal importer's.'

'Oh, him. Hugh Groton. He's a South African. He's been over here five years. He sells his animals to circuses and private collectors.'

'Did anyone check his alibi?'

'Well, actually, yes,' the AC said. 'I was here when the message came, I put Division on checking it.'

'How good was it?'

'Pretty unassailable, I'd say. He's on the committee of the Safari Club, which has premises in Kingsway. He was up there for a committee meeting and had his bed booked for two nights. The evidence is down in the minutebook. Ten people of substance can swear for him.'

'Then that's that,' Gently growled. 'How much was the tiger worth?'

'How much . . . what has that to do with it?'

'Why, everything,' Gently said, 'I'd have thought. With Groton out it can't be murder – who else could have handled a full-grown tiger? So it must be accident. Perhaps Shimpling pinched the tiger and got himelf eaten for his pains.'

The AC slowly resumed his glasses.

'Yes,' he said. 'Very ingenious, Gently.'

'I seem to remember tigers are pricey – two or three thousand for a good one.'

'And after Shimpling was eaten,' the AC said, 'did he steal his own car and bury himself? Or did the tiger do that – or maybe the milkman?'

'What's wrong with Groton having done it?'

'Groton?'

'We have to make sense of the facts. If Groton suspected what had happened, he might have reasons for keeping it dark. At the best it was a bad advert, might have led to his farm being closed. Then Shimpling may have had blackmail evidence which Groton couldn't leave lying about.

'So Groton visits the bungalow, collects the evidence, buries the remains – and pinches the car, very likely, to offset the loss of the tiger. However you tell it, it's more credible than that someone set the tiger on Shimpling. If that was the angle, why did they queer it by burying the remains and locking up?'

'Yes,' the AC said, 'yes.'

'So it's accident, not murder. They'll charge Groton

with concealing a death and pinching the car, but that's the lot.'

'Which, of course, isn't our department.'

Gently nodded approval.

'In fact all Abbotsham needs is a little phone talk – just to set them on the right track.'

'I'll ring them now.'

'Oh no you won't, Gently.'

The AC scraped back in his chair. He picked up a silver-handled paperknife and began beating his palm with it.

'I knew I was dealing with a slippery customer, but by heaven, this takes the cake! You must think I'm senile, Gently, trying to give me that load of old codswallop.

'It was a Saturday morning – remember? The morning when tradesmen knock for their money. And did one of those tradesmen go screaming to the police with a tale about a half-eaten body in a bungalow?

'They didn't, and you know why. Because they found the door locked and things tidy! While Mister Hugh Groton was still in London with umpty-ump witnesses to prove it.

'So you'll just get out of here, Gently, and you'll get in your car, and you'll drive to Abbotsham – and you'll take Inspector Dutt with you, to clear up the mess when you've finished.

'Now on your way!'

The AC stood, slammed the paperknife back on the desk.

Gently, his face still unregistering, rose more leisuredly.

'Of course, there's the Blazey case going in . . .'

'Gently,' the AC said very softly.

'And, as I said, I'm no expert on tigers . . .'

The AC was silent.

Gently left.

Outside in the passage he began to grin and was still grinning when he reached his office. Dutt was sitting with his feet on the desk and a sporting paper in his hand.

'All right,' Gently said, 'get on the blower. You won't be sleeping in Tottenham tonight. Then when you're through get me the *Daily Express*. They may have some pictures we need in their morgue.'

'Was it really about a tiger, sir?' Dutt asked.

'It was really about a tiger,' Gently said.

He went to the bookshelf and took down an encyclopaedia.

Under 'Tiger' the entry read: 'See Cats.'

CHAPTER THREE

'THAT'S THE PLACE.'

To the side of a high-hedged country road about twenty cars were pulled up with, standing about them in lounging groups, a number of hands-in-pockets men.

These were reporters. The appearance of the police car jerked them into motion. They ran to crowd round it, some lugging cameras, and a flashbulb fizzed as Gently got out.

'Chief Superintendent Gently . . . who have you brought with you? Is it a fact that Shimpling was the Cheyne-Chevington witness?'

'He was a blackmailer. May we print that?'

'Have you picked up the Banks woman?'

'Cheyne-Chevington's vanished from London. Do you know where he is?'

Already they seemed to know more about it than the police. They shouldered and pushed to get in questions, determined to have some quotes from Gently.

Behind them, guarding rusted iron gates, stood two

red-faced uniform-men, while behind the gates lay a common-place bungalow with roughcast walls and quoins of pink brick.

'What the devil do you want me to tell you? I've only arrived this minute!'

Also he was hungry and the day was close, and . . . in fact, he was ready to jump down people's throats.

'Who do you think did it – one of his victims? You can tell us that, can't you?'

'A man is involved.'

'What's his name?'

'I'll tell you later.'

'Have a heart, chiefie! Have you talked to Groton?'

'He'll be assisting us.'

'Can we quote you on that?'

'Why ask me?'

'Where was Groton the night it happened?'

'Probably minding his own business.'

Meanwhile Perkins, the chubby-faced local inspector, was prinking himself in the background, trying to give Gently the impression that he, too, was used to firing answers at a pack of reporters . . .

'All right, that's all! Let me get through.'

'There'll be a statement before lunch, won't there, chiefie?'

'Maybe yes, maybe no.'

'They'll fire us if we miss the early editions . . .'

But directly they were scattering back to their cars and taking off for the nearest phones, leaving four men to play cards and to keep a sharp eye on the bungalow.

'This is Police Constable Kennet, Super. He shot at the tiger in the Market Place.'

Previously Gently had shaken hands with Bulley, who had probably been kept after duty to meet him; now it was the turn of a gaunt-cheeked man who flushed and came raggedly to attention.

'Kennet's our demon bowler, Super. He took seven for forty-two in the Police versus Specials.'

Grunt from Gently.

'He keeps goal too. He's what you'd call an all-rounder.'

How many more were they going to trot out to shake hands with the man from the Yard?

'And this is Detective-Sergeant Gipping . . .'

A short gravel drive led up to the bungalow, branching right from the gate to a timber garage from which green paint was flaking. The gravel was scant and choked with weeds. What had once been small lawns had run away. The bungalow had two bay windows and between them a porch the door of which had a square of pebbled glass.

A dreary place. The rough-cast had greyed, the pink bricks looked immortal. Roses, smothered with grass and sending briers everywhere, lifted a scatter of apologetic blooms.

Then there were the hedges, overtopping the roof, out of which brambles had begun to encroach; and to the left of the bungalow a broken trellis was weighted down with flowering convolvulus.

Who could have wanted to live in such a place? It was a mile from the town and not on a bus route.

'Do you know who built it?'

'Sorry, Super?'

Perkins was still parading his men.

'This bungalow – who built it?'

'Oh . . . can't say I know. A local builder.'

'What I mean is, who had it built?'

Perkins didn't know this either, but Police Constable Kennet – he actually saluted – could recite the history of the bungalow.

'It was built for a bloke called Cowling, sir, he was a bit of a market-gardener. But he went broke just before the war and then the evacuees had it.

'After that it was some people called Young, but they didn't stay very long; then it was empty for a while, I remember; then I reckon this Shimping had it.'

'Did he buy the bungalow?'

'Don't know, sir. I believe he was here above a twelve-month.'

'If he didn't own it, who does?'

Nobody seemed to know that.

And there it lay, that misbegotten building, which perhaps even its builder had never loved; concealing, it might well have been for ever, the evidence of a gruesome tragedy.

'Well, let's take a look at it.'

Perkins had the key and he led the way briskly to the front door. Behind Gently came Messrs Gipping, Kennet and the rest, followed at a distance by the patient Dutt. Perkins unlocked the door and opened it cautiously.

'I'm afraid we've removed the bits and pieces . . . but

there's still plenty of stains. And the claw-marks, of course.'

Gently looked. From the front door of the bungalow the hall ran straight through to the back. Four doors opened off it, but it was unlit except by the pane in the outer door. The walls were papered with a drab flowered paper and the floor, long ago, had been painted brown.

Extending for about twelve feet inside the door was an area of thick smudged stains and savage scrapings.

'That square bit there . . . that's where we pulled up the rug. It was cemented down with blood.

'Then you can see where the chair was lying in that pool farther up.

'Look at the way those claws dug in! Poor devil, he couldn't have stood an earthly. And there, where it spouted over the wall . . .

'I was nearly sick when I first saw it.'

'Has Groton seen it?' Gently asked.

'Groton? No . . . should he have done?'

'He'd know the sort of mess a tiger makes!'

'But surely nothing else could have done it?'

Gently shrugged massively. No, there really wasn't much doubt about it! A brilliant effects-man might have faked it, but not in a hurry, straight after a killing.

And surely nobody had faked that ghastly corpse, photographs of which he had now seen . . .

'So that's where the rug came up, and that's the mark of a chair. What are those dab-marks on the fringe of the staining?'

Perkins's face became woeful. 'To tell you the truth,

I'm puzzled by them. Unless the tiger did it with his tail – you know, sort of tapped the floor with it.'

'You think that's likely?'

'Well . . . Gipping suggested it.'

'What about that curved marking, close to the wall.'

'Could he have done that with his paw?'

'And look – there's another – and another. About three feet apart.'

Perkins shook his head. 'Frankly, I'm baffled . . .'

'We'll want those marks measured and photo-graphed. I'd say chummie wore a number ten tennis shoe, but your lab-man can sort that out.'

'You mean . . . ?'

'Footprints. He was going near the wall to keep out of the blood. If he searched these two front rooms he'd have to go through it. But he found he was getting some on his shoes so he came away again on tiptoe.

'The puzzle is why there aren't more footprints – he had to fetch the body out, remember.'

Poor Perkins! He looked as dismayed as a repri-manded child. Yet it was quite obvious, the message contained in those faint marks.

And perhaps if it hadn't been so close and if Gently hadn't missed his elevenses, he'd have been more diplomatic to the well-meaning local man.

'Anyway, it doesn't tell us much. Of course, it was too late for latents?'

Perkins nodded dismally. 'We got some of the dead man's from the glass shelf in the bathroom.'

'Have you sacks or something to cover this floor? By the way, I'd like the rest of you to stay outside. Dutt,

31

prowl around and see if you can find what chummie used to shift the body.'

Then they all started to do something, except Perkins, who waited gloomily. But was it Gently's fault if he'd had this Big Man role shoved on him? The trouble was that nothing had happened at Abbotsham since the dissolution of the monasteries, and now it had they were in a flutter. You half-expected to see flags flying.

'What else have you moved from the bungalow?'

Now they were going round inside. The rooms had a doggy smell of dry rot along with a sweetish odour that was hard to place. Dismal rooms, lamentably papered, with a minimum of old, gimcrack furniture. None of the main services came out this way so the ceilings were dimmed by the fumes of oil lamps.

What sort of person had Shimpling been, to come living in a dug-out like this? Where water, pumped up by a daily stint, flowed cold from the tap unless the range was lit?

'Only the stuff out of the hall. We sent that in to the lab. There's a bureau in the next room where his papers are locked up.'

'There's a passport, is there?'

'It's an old one, expired several years ago.'

They went into what no doubt had served as the living room and was furnished with a dingy three-piece suite, also a transistor radio, which still worked, though the batteries were getting feeble.

Through the window, standing beneath bushy apple trees from which tiny unripe apples were falling, one saw a sacking screen with a uniform man posted beside it.

'How did you happen on the body?'

'Oh, that wasn't too difficult. Chummie buried it in a hurry and didn't have time to disperse the soil.'

'How deep?'

'Only a foot. You could smell it too, for matter of that.'

'Let's have the bureau undone.'

The bureau, strangely, was a good one, the only decent piece in the place. It was late-Georgian veneered mahogany with brass stringing lines and the right handles.

Perkins produced a key for it.

'We found it with the key in the lock. Everything had been rummaged out of the compartments and left in a heap inside. The drawers, too, had been turned out and the stuff shoved back anyhow.'

He pulled out the drawers and let the front down. Inside the bureau was now very tidy. Stationery was sorted off into its pigeon-holes and documents stacked neatly in the centre.

Gently went through the pile quickly – it was almost suspiciously banal. There were rate receipts going back two years, bills for fuel, clothes, tyres.

Then the passport.

Peter Dennis Shimpling, described as an author and journalist, born Guildford, England, in 1911, height 5 ft 10 in, eyes hazel, hair brown.

No special peculiarities noted, wife dash, children dash, a delicately flamboyant signature and a photograph of a man looking vaguely like Hitler.

Issued May, 1951. Visa'd in France, Switzerland, and . . .

'Have you checked through this?' Gently asked.

'Yes. It was him who was living here, all right.'

'He was in Kenya in 1953.'

'Kenya?'

'Admitted, it's a long way from South Africa.'

For a moment Perkins looked abysmally miserable, then his boyish face cleared.

'Of course! Groton comes from South Africa. That could be a connection, couldn't it?'

'It could also be a red herring, but it'll be worth following up. But what was he doing in Kenya just then . . . ? It was when the Mau–Mau were going strong.'

'I've got it. It says there he was a journalist.'

Gently shrugged. 'That could explain it.'

And Perkins was all smiles again. Really, he was a very decent fellow.

Gently pulled open drawers. They contained the usual rubbishy mixture one found in bureaus – pamphlets, old playing cards, broken pipes, loose curtain hooks and other trinkets. Also a few woman's knick-knacks – hair-clips, earrings, an empty rouge pot. Neither in the drawers nor in the top of the bureau were there any letters. Not even a postcard.

'Have you had the guts out of this?'

'How do you mean?'

Gently winked at Perkins.

'Look at this top drawer here. Notice how much shallower it is than the others?'

34

He laid the drawer on the floor then felt around inside the bureau. There was a slight click. He lifted out a small compartment attached at right angles to a piece of false lining.

'Most of them have a secret compartment, but unfortunately everyone knows it. It looks as though chummie knew about this one. But you might try it for latents.

'And there's just a chance . . .'

He began feeling again, poking up into the top of the bureau. Another click.

'Ah . . . ! This is the one he *didn't* know about.'

He brought out a flat tray, no larger than a flat-fifty cigarette-tin, with lying in it a small notebook bound in black leatherette.

'There! This is going to amuse us – Mr Shimpling's Black Book.'

'You know what it is?'

'Of course. It was bound to be here, unless chummie got his hands on it first.

'Look – dates, payments, balance carried forward. Mr Shimpling had method. The only snag is he was too cautious – just a single initial by each entry.'

'You mean they're . . . blackmail payments?'

'What else? And he was doing a snug little business. Eight, nine, ten initials, paying up as regular as company tenants. There's an H, an S, a B, a W, a C, a G, a D, an E, an L and an A, paying monthly contributions ranging from ten to fifty pounds. And no tax, don't forget.

'G was paying him twenty-five pounds.'

'G – Groton.'

'It's a pleasant thought, though it might stand for George or Gwenhylda.'

Gently felt for his pipe. For the first time the case was beginning to intrigue him a little. Already he was etching in the character of the man who'd come to live in this bungalow.

A lonely man. One familiar with human weakness, and preying on it. Who accepted his isolation as part of the game, wasn't seduced into trying to dodge it.

Coming to live in this remote spot which was yet on the fringe of his selected hunting-ground, bringing with him a woman as predatory as himself who – wasn't it probable? – helped him set up his victims.

Yes, that would be the woman's role . . . then, for some reason, she'd left.

'The Press boys think Shimpling was a queer. Did you know about that?'

'A queer?'

Perkins stared with that dismayed expression which came over his face so readily.

'But he had a woman living with him.'

'They don't have to be queer all the time.'

'No, I didn't know about that.'

And, Perkins's expression said, he didn't want to . . .

'Anyway, we'll take this book and the stuff back with us. What sort of car did Shimpling run?'

'It was a Ford Anglia. We've issued the number. Perhaps we'll get something out of that.'

They went through the kitchen door into a concrete yard, then along a path tangled with bindweed for a courtesy visit to the hole. Dutt joined them.

'I think I've found what he used. There's a garden barrow behind the garage. Right in the middle of a nettle bed – and don't those blinking nettles sting!'

'Any staining?'

Duct shook his head. 'Not with the time it's been standing out there.'

'We won't bother the lab with it, then. I just wanted to know how chummie did it.'

'Another thing, chief . . . if you'll come round the front.'

They followed him, ducking under an overblown forsythia. He led them back to the front porch and pointed to two spots at the edge of the concrete.

'See those, chief?'

They were two stars of gravel, picked clean and bright by the action of water. Seeing them, you looked automatically at the guttering. And the guttering was fractured in two places.

'What do you think, chief?'

'I think you've got it. Somebody backed a truck in and damaged the gutter.'

'That's my idea, they used a truck. They'd have had the doors off and just touched the two places.'

Gently turned to Perkins. 'How does Groton shift his livestock?'

Perkins swallowed. 'A truck, of course! He had it waiting when the tiger was loose – a big closed truck with barred windows.'

'Then maybe we've solved one problem.'

At a distance, Gipping and Kennet were poring over the wheelbarrow.

The four reporters had paused in their card-playing and were now all staring intently towards the bungalow.

CHAPTER FOUR

A T LUNCH THE same atmosphere of occasion prevailed. The locals had taken him a room in the Angel Inn, the status hotel in Abbotsham.

It was a large, handsome coaching inn with an archway leading into a big yard. Dickens had stayed there, from which it was presumed that 'Eatanswill' was modelled on Abbotsham; and a Georgian house round the corner was identified as his Academy for Young Ladies.

'Dickens stayed here, you know . . .'

It was the conversation piece at lunch. Instead of being allowed to enjoy himself, Gently was being feted in a private dining room.

On his right hand sat the chief constable, a craggy-faced man with accusing eyes; on his left a Superintendent Bradfield, who claimed to have known Gently when the latter was a detective-sergeant.

Starting with iced lemon, they had gone through a menu much too substantial for a warm day, accompanied by wine which Gently would gladly have swapped for a chaste glass of lager. Then there was cognac with the coffee, poured by the chief constable himself, and finally over-large cigars from a box served on a silver salver. And:

'Dickens stayed here, you know . . .'

It was the other thing that had happened at Abbotsham!

'We got them to put you in the Pickwick suite. There's a "Pickwick" in the lounge with the passages marked.'

He had grunted into his cigar. He was sweating, his head was swimming from all the drink. While, as for solving the Shimpling affair, he could see that nobody cared about that . . .

'What's it like, working in the Central Office?'

This, a little wistfully, from Superintendent Brad-field.

'Perhaps you'd care to drop in this evening and meet the missus . . . she's always been a big fan of yours.'

Was it ever going to break up? There seemed no getting through those fiendish cigars. At the other end of the table, grinning broadly, Dutt was holding court with Perkins and Gipping.

Finally, with the clock pushing three, the chief constable sighed and scraped back his chair.

He'd dated Gently for the evening, but now they'd have to fill in with some blasted routine . . .

'You coming to Headquarters?'

'Yes. I've calls to make.'

'Drive you there. I've got to look in.'

So, in the estate-wagon, to HQ, where he frowned

and sweated as he talked to the Yard; the stink of that cigar still in his nostrils, and a thick head beginning to develop.

Well . . . he was only there for forty-eight hours . . . just shouldering the Yard's public image for it!

'I've put them on finding the blonde for us . . . she'll probably know who those initials refer to. Though whether she'll talk . . . also Cheyne-Chevington. That's a shot in the dark. And a query about Groton.'

'Do you think he has form, chief?'

'I'm sure he hasn't. Or we'd have shunted him back to SA. But the Foreign Office might know something, like what he was doing in 53.'

'If he was in Kenya along with Shimpling—'

'Come on. We'll talk to the man himself.'

Groton's farmhouse was at the end of a lane joining a major road from Abbotsham to Hawkshill. The road ran westward and left the town by a steep incline crested with trees.

They drove for ten minutes. At the top of the lane appeared a notice board painted in red and white. It read:

HUGH GROTON
ZOOLOGICAL SUPPLIER
It Is Dangerous To Trespass Here
KEEP OUT!

They drove down the lane, which ran straight and ended in a pair of gates made from steel tube. Perkins, who was driving, sent Gipping to open them, then drove through into a gravelled yard.

41

'Does Groton live here alone?' Gently asked.

'As far as we know,' Perkins said. 'I wouldn't like to vouch for who he brings out here. I'm told he goes after the women.'

'What about staff?'

'A couple of farm-workers. A wife of one of them sees to the house for him.'

'Where do they live?'

'They come from Hawkshill. They cycle in each day.'

The yard was bounded by the brick wall of an outbuilding by which grew nettles and a big elder. To its left, through a small metal gate which stood open, a path ran to the door of the straw-thatched farmhouse.

The door stood open also. A man came out.

'That's Groton . . .' Perkins muttered.

Groton had seen the car and was coming towards it, carrying a double-barrelled shotgun under his arm. On recognizing the identity of the car he stopped, then came on again, the gun held slacker.

'So it's you lot again!'

Gently had never before seen a man so massive. Groton stood six feet two or three and had the chest and shoulders of a gorilla.

An immense man! He wore an army shirt and jodhpurs tucked into vast bush-boots. The weight of him made the gravel crunch loudly, you almost expected to feel the ground tremble.

'Why didn't you give me a ring? You know how I feel about visitors.'

Above a bull-neck was set a black-maned head and a broad-featured face with huge cheekbones.

'One day I'll put a stockade round the place.'

Deep-set grey eyes, a hooked nose, a vast jaw.

'I'll buy a consignment of prickly pear, that'll put a stop to you. What do you want?'

Gently got out. For once in his life he was feeling physically insignificant. His hefty six feet, alongside Groton, diminished to the scale of lightweight humanity.

That gun, for instance, in Groton's paws . . . it looked about the size of a gaming pistol!

'You're Groton?'

'Who the devil else?'

'I'm Chief Superintendent Gently, Central Office.'

'So what do I do – throw a fit?'

'I want to have a look at that truck you use.'

They stared at each other. Perhaps it was the high cheekbones that made Groton's grey eyes so narrow. There were streaks of white in his black hair but it shone with a liberal dressing of oil.

Then he laughed, a yokellish guffaw.

'Right you are, Mr Chief Superintendent. If you want to see the truck, you can. Just watch out you don't finish up inside it.'

Was it a threat or a jest? The grey eyes glittered at Gently a moment longer. Then Groton laughed again and swung away, pounding across the gravel with grinding boots.

They followed. He led them round the outbuilding into what had previously been a cattle-yard, a drained rectangle of concrete enclosed by byres with halved doors.

From the byres came scufflings and yelpings and a faint, straw-like smell of animals, and in a dark doorway closed with steel mesh a striped face appeared suddenly, then vanished.

'Feeling nervous?' Groton leered. 'There're some funny customers round here. Wolves. Lynxes. A mountain leo. It doesn't take a big cat to wipe your face off.'

'Don't you get nervous?' Gently asked.

Groton bellowed his laughter. 'You're a comic,' he said. 'I'm a cat-man, you read me? I've got what it takes. I can stroke a tigger, and he'll purr.

'There's 'phant-men and snake-men, and I've met one who could charm rhinos. But I'm a cat-man, feller. They go with me. We're pals.'

'And cats are all you deal in?' Gently said.

'Nope. I didn't say that.'

Groton halted, made a sweeping motion with the hand that held the gun.

'What do you want? A pair of zees? I can sell you a couple for twelve-fifty. A couple of zees look good strutting around in your paddock.

'Or how about some roos – you can talk roos to your pals for hours. Or maybe a brace of spider-monkeys. If you've a hot-house, that is.'

'How much would a tiger cost?'

'Tiggers are for millionaires, feller. Do you know what it costs to run a tigger? Around fifty a week, over a period. You come across the three H's – that's heat, horse-meat and hired hands. Then there's insurance, overheads and vets. You won't see change out of fifty.'

'But how much would one cost?'

Groton frowned.

'Say three thou. That's what I was going to ask for the tigger they shot last year.'

'Who was your customer?'

'Patsy Morris. He's the Canadian lumber-king, you know? He's got a ranch and a private zoo in Perthshire. I've sold him leos and some big monks.'

'Where else could you sell one?'

'You tell me. I've only sold one tigger in five years.'

Groton strode on.

They entered a compound with an open-sided machinery shed adjoining it. In the shed stood a Vauxhall estate car and a closed truck painted dark green. The truck had very small windows of reinforced glass set behind grids of slim bars and beneath the windows, stencilled in red, the legend:

WILD ANIMALS — KEEP AWAY!

Groton waved to it.

'Take a good look. I invented the loading gear myself.'

'How long have you had this truck?'

'Since I started in business. They're damned expensive things to buy.'

Gently went in, walked round the truck. At the rear it was closed by a tailboard and two doors. Both tailboard and doors were fitted to pintles from which they simply slid or lifted off. The pintles stood proud by about two inches from the framing of the walls and floor.

'Dutt . . .'

'Yes, chief.'

Dutt pulled out a rule and began to take measurements. Groton came and leaned against a timber support, watching, whistling through his teeth.

'What's the arrangement behind the doors?' Gently asked.

'I'll show you when sonny has finished fooling.'

Dutt scribbled down figures, then nodded to Gently.

'Right,' Gently said.

Groton opened the doors and dropped the tailboard, revealing a heavy diamond grille. The grille descended into a slot in the steel floor of the truck where it was retained by four bolts. The truck wails were lined with corrugated steel and the floor was stainless steel with a diamond tread. The windows were also barred inside and there was a window looking into the cab.

Groton clouted the grille with his fist.

'Take a look at that . . . patents pending.'

'The doors and the tailboard – are they strictly necessary?'

Groton guffawed. 'Not for keeping in the livestock! But they need to be warm and out of draughts – there's heat laid on from the engine. And people don't like tiggers staring at them. Makes them nervous, you know?'

'How do you raise and lower the grille?'

'Remote control from the cab.'

'How would you load a tiger in there?'

'Now you're asking for trade secrets.'

Groton took out a cigar, bit the end off it. He blew a tornado of smoke at Gently and rubbed the match to fragments between thumb and finger.

'I know the idea you're getting, feller. Someone used the truck to pinch the tigger. But it's not on. You know why? They couldn't load it, for a start.'

'Somehow it got to the other side of town.'

'That's no distance for a tigger.'

'Nobody saw it on the way there.'

'It would have gone round, through the fields.'

'But why did it go where it went?'

Groton shook his head, made the cigar crackle.

'You don't know tiggers. They're curious beasts. They don't quite figure like the other 'mals.

'A tigger's got brains. Not brains like us, but a darned sight more than a leo. You know pretty well how a leo will act, but it's fatal to guess about a tigger.

'You just keep watching them, that's all. If you try to out-think them – feller, you're dead!'

'Still, it would be six miles to that bungalow.'

'A tigger could do it in fifteen minutes.'

'Who else drives the truck besides you?'

'Nobody. The hired hands don't drive.'

'And nobody but you could load the tiger?'

Groton blew a lot more smoke.

'Look, feller,' he said. 'I've people to vouch for me. I wasn't there when the tigger went.

'I was in town. Don't say you haven't checked me. I never stirred out of the Club. We had a committee from seven thirty and then supper and then a booze.

'I went to bed about one a.m. and I shared a room

47

with another member. The keys of this truck were in my pocket – it never shifted out of the compound.'

'Can tigers open doors?' Gently said.

'To hell with tiggers and doors!'

'This one must have opened a door. Then locked it again when it left.'

Groton glared at Gently, his huge hands clenching. He had the cigar between his teeth.

Beside him, looking unusually diminutive, Dutt stood under-scoring figures in his notebook.

'That tiger left here in the truck,' Gently said. 'There's no doubt about that. The truck was driven to the bungalow and backed up to it and then the tiger released.

'If nobody else could load the tiger there's only one other alternative. You left it ready loaded for someone before you went to London.'

'Did I hell!'

'Then what happened?'

'How should I know what happened?'

'It's the other way round, Mr Groton. How could you *not* know what happened?'

Groton was sweating. A film gleamed on the creased skin of his brow, dark patches were showing beneath the arms of the khaki shirt.

It was too easy . . .

Gently glanced at Perkins, standing unhappy-faced to his right. Probably he was cursing himself for not having a go before the Yard men were called in . . .

'I've seen the statement you made at that time. You say you left the farm at six p.m. That was after your employees left to cycle home to Hawkshill.'

'I didn't load up that tigger.'

'But nobody else could have done, you tell me.'

'They could if they knew how.'

'You mean, if you'd given them instruction?'

'No!'

Groton threw down the cigar and rasped it to shreds under his boot.

'All right, I was shooting a line about that. It only takes savvy to figure it out.

'You dump some horse-meat in the truck and back the truck up to the cage. The cage has a porch with a ramp at the same level as the floor of the truck. Then you open the cage doors – they slide – and raise the grille from the cab.

'When tigger comes in you drop the grille, and that's it. Tigger's loaded.'

'Sounds simple,' Gently said.

'Didn't I say I was shooting a line?'

'All it needs is someone who knew about the truck and about you being away, and who had some horse-meat.'

'I can't help what it needed!'

'You don't like to tell us who it was?'

Groton dragged his fingers through his black mane.

'Feller,' he said, 'don't push me like that.'

But his big face had a greyish look and his eyes were pulling away from Gently. Sweat was trickling through the dark hairs of his chest which showed through the unbuttoned shirt.

He knew. He must know.

At least, he must have a suspicion!

Somebody familiar with the farm, who'd hung about there, watched animals handled . . .

'What were you doing before you came over here?'

Back in the old cattle-yard something set up a howl.

'I was a pro, what do you think? A hunter. Never been anything else.'

'Where, exactly . . . ?'

'All over. Up in 'Yika for a long while.'

'In Kenya?'

'Who said Kenya?'

'Tanganyika is next door to it.'

Groton hesitated. 'So what?' he said. 'I've been all over. Kenya too.'

'Were you there in 1953?'

Another pause. 'Could have been.'

'Was it safe for hunting just then?'

'As safe as it ever is with greenhorns!'

'There was Mau–Mau trouble,' Gently said. 'It was big news. It brought the pressmen.'

'I'm a hunter, I wasn't news.'

'It brought Peter Shimpling.'

'He should have stayed there.'

Gently felt in his pocket, drew out an envelope. Groton watched him with slitted eyes. Gently took three photographs from the envelope and handed them to Groton.

'Do you know these people?'

Groton barely glanced at the photographs.

'Never met them in my life.'

'I suggest you take a good look at them.'

'How is that going to help?'

50

But he lowered his eyes to look at the photographs, as though doing his best to identify them. They were press pictures of Dr Cheyne-Chevington, Shimpling and Shirley Banks.

Shimpling here looked very respectable. He wore a bowler and carried an umbrella. Cheyne-Chevington was scowling as he got into a car. Shirley Banks had posed brassily for the cameraman.

'What about this one with the little moustache . . . ?'

'Aren't I telling you? I don't know them.'

'Give him a topee with a press pass stuck in it . . . sunglasses . . . a linen jacket . . .'

'No!'

'You never met him?'

'If I did I don't remember.'

'Kenya . . . 1953 . . . ?'

'Who says I did?'

'Did you?'

'No!'

'It's Shimpling, of course,' Gently said. 'I think you must have run across him. He was living here for eighteen months. He'd perhaps want to chat about Kenya . . .'

Groton shoved the photographs back at Gently.

'Look, I've had enough of this palava! If you've nothing better to do, get to hell off my farm.'

Gently nodded.

'I'll want to talk to your men.'

'Then ruddy talk to them – and get out!'

Gently nodded again, didn't say anything.

Groton snatched up his gun and slammed away across the compound.

Perkins came forward.

'May I see those photographs . . . ?'

Dutt was closing his notebook and grinning.

Where Groton had gone there was a sudden scuffling and snarling, then a chilling, high-pitched whine.

Perkins said: 'This fellow here, just getting into the car . . .'

He made his face of misery.

'I think I know him,' he said.

CHAPTER FIVE

B UT THEY GOT little out of the two countrymen who assisted Groton with his animals. They were elderly men who probably found mucking-out cages an easier task than hedging and ditching.

'Don't ask us how that varmint got out . . . we never had a lot to do with him. Mr Groton, he sees to the big 'uns. You wouldn't catch us going in there like he do . . .'

Two easy-going men with placid eyes, strangely similar in feature, reflecting, as though they were mirrors, the sunny fields to which they belonged. Jimma Cook and Harbut Reeves. Growing old with the greenness of country things.

'Do you remember when you left that night?'

Gently had found them wheeling in litter. Now they stood around in the shade of an elder tree from which the sun drew a pungent odour.

'Ha'past five is our time, less there's anything want doing. Mr Groton's a turn nut but he isn't a bad man to work for.'

'Did anything special happen that day?'

'I don't recall . . . what do you say, Jimma?'

'Not unless he was fussin' a bit about getting away to his meeting.'

'How was he fussing?'

'Well, you know. He was a bit niggly to get them all fed.'

'Who fed the tiger?'

'Blast, we didn't. We never liked getting too close to that.'

'Was the tiger fed that day?'

'I s'pose it was . . . don't you, Harbut?'

'He fed it in the morning, I know. I watched him. I was kept too busy in the afternune . . .'

What shone through it all, unexpectedly, was a sort of affection for Groton; he was just the biggest and most intriguing of the animals on the farm. With them, he might have dropped from another planet, so inconceivable was his origin. Jimma and Harbut viewed him uncritically – a rum nut, but not necessarily a bad 'un.

'Did Jimma's missus go home with you two?'

'No, she's away at ha'past three. She get his dinner and see to things – we have our dinner in the kitchen with him.'

'Does he have many visitors?'

'No, not him. He don't like people round the farm. And another thing hangs to it, what's more – there's not a lot of people want to come round here.'

'But he has some visitors?'

'Ah, now and then.'

'Such as . . . ?'

'Customers. He'll have them in.'

'Doesn't he have any friends here?'

'Not very often.'

'Just take a look at these photographs.'

They looked at the photographs, as at all else, with an unhurried contemplation; but photographs were not of their world and they returned them at last without comment.

Harbut remembered a visitor who had looked at the tiger, it may have been a week before the escape, but recalled only that he was smartish-looking and drove a posh kind of car.

'He was having a long talk with Mr Groton, but I didn't pay any attention. They was round the tiger's cage for a while. Then they went and sat in Mr Groton's car.'

Gently thanked them and they stood watching while the four policemen walked away.

A movement behind a window in the farmhouse suggested that Groton was watching too . . .

They drove towards town. Perkins was more unhappy than Gently had seen him yet. He sat hunched in a corner in the back of the police car trying desperately to jog his memory.

'I'm sure I've seen that man somewhere . . .'

Gipping had seen the photograph without recognizing it. But Cheyne-Chevington's face, though rather handsome, had very little to distinguish it.

'Of course, it may not have been in Abbotsham. I get about a bit in the district. Or perhaps I'm just remembering that photograph — what did it appear in, the *Express*?'

Gently shrugged, but didn't press him. Why worry? It would work out. The shape of the business was being established, the details would come in their own good time.

Perhaps not in his time — he was handing over tomorrow.

But Dutt and Perkins, between them, could have a ball tying it up . . .

'Let's run over the facts as we know them to date.'

In other words, make certain they were getting the picture!

'Groton and Shimpling were in Kenya together in 1953, and I'm pretty sure there was some funny business, though we don't know what.

'Shimpling was there as a journalist. We'll have some details of that shortly. Groton was presumably leading a safari, or he might have been collecting animals to sell.

'Seven years later Shimpling is police witness in a drug-trafficking case against Cheyne-Chevington: the case was laid on evidence volunteered by Shimpling and by a prostitute, Shirley Banks.

'It failed, but as a result of it Cheyne-Chevington was struck off. The defence claimed that Cheyne-Chevington had been blackmailed by Shimpling but they could offer no evidence. The police, however, had strong suspicions that Shimpling was indeed a blackmailer.

'Within nine months of that trial Shimpling is living

in the bungalow here with Shirley Banks, only a few miles from the farm where Groton has established an animal-supplying business.

'That business is a profitable one. Groton has given us an instance. At different times he has told us he bought the tiger for seven hundred and fifty, and that he proposed to sell it to a Canadian millionaire for three thousand.

'Even allowing for acclimatization and training, that would leave a handsome profit.

'Shimpling continues his blackmail activity. We have evidence of it in his "black book". He is drawing money from a number of sources, among others from one designated "G".

'This continues for eighteen months during most of which time he has Banks living with him; then Banks leaves, and soon after that we have the affair with the tiger – on the very night when Groton has an alibi which nobody can question.

'Investigation shows that a truck was used and that the truck almost certainly was Groton's; also that Groton had an opportunity to load the tiger before he left for London; also that shortly before he was visited by a man who was interested in the tiger, and who had a long talk with Groton; and that the murderer searched the bungalow and probably found and destroyed the blackmail evidence.

'Those are the facts.

'You can safely add to them that Groton is a liar.'

He stared hard at Perkins, but Perkins obviously hadn't been listening.

With head bowed, the local man was still wrestling with his memory . . .

Dutt said: 'I reckon there was two of them, chief. It'd have been dicey for one man to do that job.'

Gently grunted and got out his pipe.

Perkins murmured: 'It's his expression . . . I remember the expression.'

Outside Headquarters they ran into the pressmen, who had somehow lost track of them during the lunch break. Now they came running over to the car as Gipping parked it in a slot.

'We've something for you, chiefie – a bit of info about Shimpling.'

'Meet Harry – Harry Barnes'

'Harry's freelance for Smith's PA.'

They pushed an elderly, dark-jowled man towards him and immediately flashbulbs began to pop. This was news at all events – a pressman telling the Yard something.

'So what's this info?'

'I was working with Shimpling. He was at Smith's PA for a while.'

When?'

''Fifty-two, 'fifty-three. We were in Paris together.'

'Lucky for you. What then?'

'They sent him to Nairobi to cover Mau-Mau. He was out there six months. Then he dropped out of sight.'

'How do you mean?'

'He left Smith's. He hasn't been newsing for anyone since.'

'Sure?'

'Pretty sure. Someone would have heard if he had.'

'And Groton was out that way,' somebody put in. 'He was a hunter before he came to England.'

'Shimpling might have had something on him.'

'There's your tie-up for you, chiefie.'

Gently looked from one to another of them.

'Thank you,' he said. 'Now I can go home. Just tell me how a man can be juggling with tigers at Abbotsham while he's sitting in a club in Kingsway.'

'Is Groton in the clear then?' came from all over.

'No comment on Groton.'

'Oh, give us a break, chiefie.'

'Groton has been assisting us. We think his truck was used. And you can print what you like about Shimpling and Kenya.'

Once more, as soon as they were certain they'd got all he was going to give them, they dashed away to talk it up into a story on the phones.

Meanwhile Superintendent Bradfield, who'd watched complacently from the steps, smiled deprecatingly and murmured:

'The Yard have been on the phone for you . . .'

They went with him into his office, a large room smelling of varnish, at a table in which a plain-clothes man was typing on a machine with a double carriage.

'This is Sergeant Hargrave—'

'What extension was it?'

'Oh. Extension one-seven.'

Sergeant Hargrave, who had bobbed to his feet, sat down again, but didn't dare go on with his typing.

Gently took the swivel-chair at the desk, dialled and asked for the extension. Bradfield, Perkins and Gipping stood by the desk like three naughty boys up for a wigging.

'That you, Ferrow?'

'Ferrow here, chief.'

'Have you picked up Banks yet?'

'Divisions are working on it, chief. They haven't come up with anything yet.'

'What have you got?'

'About Shimpling, chief. He worked as a journalist at one time.'

'I know.'

'He was sent to Kenya—'

'I know. Skip Shimpling. What about Groton?'

'Just a minute, chief. A confidential report . . .'

Everything from the Foreign Office was confidential! Gently stared woodenly across the desk while he listened to Ferrow playing around with some papers.

'Here we are. He was born in Griqualand—'

'Never mind about Griqualand.'

'Well . . . he's been fined twice for ill-treating natives and once for poaching game in the Kruger National Park. Suspected connection with ivory-poaching but no charge brought. Another fine for tax-dodging and one for the illicit sale of a firearm.'

'Nothing big?'

'There's a sealed envelope stamped "For Your Eyes Only".'

'Open it, for heaven's sake!'

'Thought I'd better ask you, chief.'

Further pause, with background sounds of Ferrow dealing with the envelope. Bradfield, after jiffling for a moment, pulled up a chair and sat down on it awkwardly.

Bradfield . . . Gently remembered him now: he'd been a detective constable in those days. A bland-faced youngster, fresh off the beat, who'd picked up a man in a shooting incident.

Now he was Super, running his own show, smitten with the glamour of the Yard . . .

'Hello, chief?'

'What's the big secret?'

'Something to do with the Mau-Mau business.'

'Is it, by heaven!'

'In 53. That's when—'

'I know. Just stick to the facts.'

'It was in August 53 at a place called M'Butu, Northern Province. Somebody burned a Kikuyu village and shot eight of the natives.

'There was an inquiry. Groton was there. He was staying at a game farm three miles off. The night before some animals were slaughtered and one of the boys had his head cut off.

'The inquiry was closed for lack of evidence and the burning was blamed on rival tribes, but the authorities are convinced it was done by white men and that Groton was the instigator.

'He was given a one-way ticket and the affair was hushed up.'

'No mention of journalists nosing round?'

'Sorry, chief. Nothing about that.'

'Do we know the dates of Shimpling's visit?'

'He was there from March till September.'

So there it was, dovetailing neatly, just as he had been certain it would: the connection between the blackmailing Shimpling and the fierce but vulnerable South African.

What evidence had Shimpling collected in Africa?

That they were never likely to know.

Unless, perhaps, the Banks woman had been privy to the secret . . .

But one thing was becoming clear – Groton was a very slippery customer. The English police, like their Kenya counterparts, might be reduced to issuing a one-way ticket . . .

'Tell them I want Banks and want her quickly.'

'Willco, chief. It shouldn't take long.'

'It's taken too long already!'

He could sense Ferrow shrugging his shoulders.

'Also I want a check on Cheyne-Chevington. I'd like to know where he's living.'

'Matthews has been checking for you, chief, but he hasn't picked up the trail so far.'

Gently hung up.

Bradfield met his eye with an interrogating smile.

'Everything all right . . . ?'

The man was an ass! Gently had an impulse to say something rude.

Over by the door, a shrinking violet, hovered the uniformed figure of Police Constable Kennet. He made a sort of inclination as Gently's eye fell on him and shuffled forward a couple of steps.

'Excuse me, sir . . .'

'What is it?'

'It's something that came to me, sir. About the bungalow and who owns it. I thought it might be of use to you.'

'Well?'

'Hastings handled it, sir.'

'Who are Hastings?'

'They're estate agents. They've an office in the Buttermarket, sir. I look in their window when I'm passing.'

'And they advertised the bungalow?'

'Yes, sir. It came back to me, I'd seen the card in their window . . .'

Kennet broke off. Inspector Perkins had suddenly come out of his long trance. He was quivering in his excitement and exclaimed:

'That's him! It's David Hastings!'

Everyone turned to him, and he flushed. But he kept on repeating enthusiastically:

'It's David Hastings – the man with the car! I *knew* I recognized him! It's David Hastings!'

CHAPTER SIX

P RECISELY AT THAT moment the phone went – it
was Matthews wanting to give Gently a personal
report; and then Ferrow came back on the line with a
report from Divisions about Shirley Banks.

Both reports were entirely negative, but of course,
Gently was expected to listen!

While over his head Perkins kept expostulating and
Bradfield chimed in his amazement and incredulity.

'We'd better be careful about this, Perky . . .'

'No, I'm positive – it's the expression! He's got a
little beard, now, and a moustache, but a man can't
alter his expressions.'

'. . . he simply faded out from Kensington, chief. A
man called Beevor took over the practice . . .'

'You'd expect he'd try to alter his appearance, after
all . . .'

'We don't want to stir up trouble locally . . .'

For five minutes the babel went on, then Gently
hung up and everyone fell silent.

Perkins, red in the face, was staring bulbously at the

lino; Bradfield tapped his foot, wore a doubting expression.

'Well . . . ?'

Perkins swallowed. 'May I see the picture again?'

Gently produced it and they all clustered round. Plainly nobody else was prepared to go nap on it, though Kennet kept nodding his head cautiously.

'What do you think?'

'It's the expression, really! I know there's not much to go on in the face . . .'

'What about the rest of you?'

Kennet shuffled his feet.

Bradfield said: 'I don't know the man myself . . .'

'When did Hastings arrive here?' Gently asked.

'He hasn't been here long,' Bradfield said. 'It used to be Sayers who had the business — Samuel Sayers. I bought my place through him.'

'How long ago was that?'

'March 59 . . . over four years. It couldn't have been long after that when it changed hands, though Sayers was living here till recently. There's a flat over the business. Sayers lived in that. He was a bachelor.'

'He had some form, sir,' Gipping said. 'Soliciting men for immoral purposes.'

'Where is he now?'

'He's slung his hook, sir. I wouldn't know where he's gone to.'

Gently nodded. It had a promising sound; Shimpling had also been a queer. And along with the 'G' in the 'black book' there had been an 'H' and an 'S'.

'Is he a married man, your David Hastings?'

After the trial, Cheyne-Chevington's wife had left him.

'No, he's a bachelor too,' Perkins said. 'He used to live in a service-flat opposite my house. That's why I know what he looks like, I'd see him going in and out. The wife says he had girls there. But he was living on his own.'

'Where's he living now?'

Perkins looked unhappy. 'Somewhere in the town.'

'When did he move?'

'Last year some time. Now it's an accountant who lives there.'

'What else do you know about him?'

'That's about all. He seems to have plenty of money – dresses well, runs a Jag. Does a lot of advertising in the *Free Press*.'

'Does he know Groton?'

Perkins shook his head. 'But it's him all right, I'm sure of that.'

He fixed his gaze rigidly on the photograph as though willing Cheyne-Chevington to be Hastings.

Bradfield said quickly: 'I wouldn't want to upset him, not unless we're positive, that is. Abbotsham's a small place really . . . we try not to play things tough, here.'

Of course. Abbotsham had tone!

'Somebody was playing it tough last year . . .'

'Oh, I'm not trying to make obstacles!'

'Good. I think we'd better talk to Mr Hastings.'

Bradfield bit his lip and looked slantingly, but raised no other objection.

They crossed the Buttermarket: Gently and Perkins, with Dutt following behind.

It was a broad, lazy street proceeding from one corner of the Market Place.

Cars were double-parked along one side, which was blocked at the top by a projecting building, so that the street had the aspect of a narrow plain which was only partly a thoroughfare.

It was lined by a variety of decorative fronts of Georgian and early Victorian origin, dwelling-houses which had since been converted to shops and offices. Some, on the side used only for parking, still had sweeps of steps with wrought-iron railings.

Looking towards the Market Place, you saw the gabled flint front of the Jew's House.

'This area would be rather expensive?'

Perkins nodded. 'Yes. All round here. When these places come up for sale it's usually a chain store that buys them.'

'Which is Hastings?'

'Behind the cars. You can see the gold lettering on the windows. But nobody owns anything along this side, they're all on lease from an insurance company.'

Rather surprisingly, the building which contained Hastings was of Edwardian red-brick, a double-fronted doll's house of a place loaded with rococo ornament.

Yet, perhaps because the ornamentation was so thorough-going, so enthusiastically ebullient, the house had charm and didn't seem out of place.

A voluptuously-curved brass plate was mounted on the multiple flutings of the porch.

It read:

DAVID HASTINGS
Property Agent
Late S. M. L. Sayers
Late Alistair Upley

A massively panelled door stood open, held by a green glass doorstop.

They went in.

Through swing doors was an office bisected by a long counter. A girl seated behind the counter was entering duplicated sheets in a big box-file.

The walls were fitted with sections of peg-board each of which was covered with photographs of properties and behind the counter hung framed architects' plans and elevations.

Everything was new and up to date. The office smelled faintly of plastic file-envelopes.

The girl was pretty and smartly dressed and came forward with a smile.

'Can I help you?'

'We'd like to see Mr Hastings.'

'If it's about a property on the books—'

'No. We want to see him personally.'

'In that case . . . have you an appointment?'

'No. No appointment.'

'What is your name, sir, please?'

Gently paused. 'George Gently.'

She picked up a jade-green phone and spoke into it deferentially. As she listened her eyes flickered, took in Gently, fell away.

'If you'll go up the stairs, sir . . . Mr Hastings will see you.'

They went up a plastic-treaded stairway with mahogany banisters. At the top was a wide landing, freshly painted in light colours, and across it a door with frosted-glass panels on which was gilded: David Hastings.

Gently knocked. They entered. A man had risen to his feet. He'd been sitting behind a big sapele-wood desk, but now he came round it towards them.

'Mr . . . Gently?'

'Chief Superintendent Gently.'

'Yes! I felt there couldn't be two of you.'

'You're David Hastings?'

'Who else?'

'I'm investigating the murder of Peter Shimpling.'

Their eyes met. Hastings was a tallish man with sloping shoulders and an elegant figure. He wore a quiet, stylish lounge suit that accentuated his narrow waist.

He had dark hair and bluish eyes and unobtrusively handsome features; his small beard was pointed sharply and his moustache trimmed close.

His eyes had a tired sort of humour.

'You think I can help you with that in some way?'

'That's why we are here.'

'You surprise me, but never mind. Close the door and find yourselves seats.'

69

He went back to the desk and picked up the phone.

'Anne, I'm busy till I ring again . . .'

Then he sat down, crossing his feet, letting his hands fall naturally on his lap.

'Go ahead.'

'First, look at these.'

Out came the photographs again. Hastings spread them across the desk and looked at each of them amusedly.

'Do I know these people?'

'I'm asking you.'

'That fellow there is my double.'

'Just your double?'

'People have them, you know. Who is he – what's he done?'

He stared steadily at Gently, the bored twinkle never faltering.

All the other chairs in the room were low ones, and the desk sited with its back to the window.

'He's a man I want to talk to,' Gently said. 'His name is Miles Cheyne-Chevington. He was a doctor who supplied cocaine to prostitutes. He was struck off the Register in 1960.'

'I remember the case,' Hastings said.

Not once did his eyes waver.

'But surely it was brought on framed evidence, and the verdict given was Not Guilty?'

Gently said nothing.

Hastings tapped the photograph. 'And now you think he might be me?'

'Do you deny it?'

'But of course.'

'Can you prove your identity?'

'Can you disprove it?'

Gently said: 'If you are not that man you can easily help me by proving your identity. You can produce your birth certificate, for instance, your stamp card, your passport.'

'And if I don't?'

'Why shouldn't you? That's the question I'll ask myself.'

'It might be I don't like impertinent inquiries, even from a chief superintendent.'

Hastings smiled. He'd given the flick without the smallest edge of animosity – almost professionally, like a counsel who had a lunch date with his opponent.

'Right,' Gently said. 'Let's look at some facts. The Cheyne-Chevington trial was three years ago. Three years ago you bought this business. Where did you come from, to Abbotsham?'

'Does it matter?'

'You don't want to tell me?'

'Is it compulsory for me to tell you?'

'We can check on these things, Mr Hastings.'

'Then why bother me with them, Superintendent?'

Again, no animosity! Just a lawyer-like non sequitur . . . Didn't he realize he could never win this sort of game with the police?

'You say you remember the Cheyne-Chevington case.'

'Clearly. It had good coverage in the gutter-press.'

'Then you'll remember that Shimpling was involved in it – was, in fact, the principal witness?'

'Oh yes.'

'You don't know Shimpling?'

'I don't remember setting eyes on him.'

'Not in this office?'

Hastings hesitated. 'I have a lousy memory for faces.'

'Did you or didn't you?'

Hastings said smoothly: 'Now you jog my memory, I believe I must have done. That bungalow of his was on our books. It was a property we inherited from Sam Sayers.'

'I'm glad you remember that,' Gently said. 'Even though your memory for faces is so bad. In fact, Shimpling bought the bungalow through you?'

'Yes.'

'Perhaps you'll tell me about the transaction?'

For the first time Hastings dropped his eyes, but it was only for a moment. As though he'd looked away to give himself a pause to recall something remote . . .

'Of course, I'm a property agent, not a solicitor . . . you do appreciate the difference? I merely bring people who want to sell into contact with people who want to buy.'

'Meaning?'

'My interest in a transaction is limited. It ends when I collect my commission. In the circumstances it would be academic to retain a complete file of records.'

'Are you telling me you've no record of this transaction?'

'I think it very unlikely. At a pinch I might look up the entry made when the commission was received.'

'They, you'll know who conveyed the property.'

'I'm not so certain of that.'

'And you'll know who were the vendors.'

'I'm afraid I've forgotten long since.'

'I see,' Gently said. 'No records, no memories. About what one would expect to find if there were no conveyance either.'

'No conveyance . . . ?'

'Between Shimpling and the vendors.'

Hastings laughed politely. 'I'm not with you . . .

'Isn't it plain? You don't have any records because Shimpling never did buy the bungalow.'

Hastings's eyes went suddenly flat, then just as suddenly regained their expression. He leaned back and made a humouring gesture with his hand.

'But that's ridiculous! I drew a commission. There's no doubt about the sale—'

'Listen to me! You've made a mistake, and now you can see where it's led you.

'If you're Hastings you can produce those records and tell us who conveyed the property to Shimpling. If you can't, as far as I'm concerned you are Miles Cheyne-Chevington.

'Because if Shimpling didn't buy that property, there's no doubt how he obtained it. By blackmail. By blackmailing you. And the conveyance will show that you were the purchaser.

'Now – do we get the records, or do we assume you are Cheyne-Chevington?'

'I've told you, I don't remember—'

Gently shook his head. 'You remember! A body has been dug up in that property – that would have set your memory working.

'The body of a client is dug up in a property you sold him less than three years back. Wouldn't you have been thinking about it, talking about it, remembering every detail of the business?'

'That may be so, but nevertheless—'

'You pretended just now that you hadn't. It was only when you guessed we knew that you'd handled the property that you decided to "remember".'

'Let me remind you—'

'No! Do we get the records, or don't we?'

Silence. David Hastings sat fingering his neat beard. He had a mobile, thin-lipped mouth, and now the corners of the mouth were dragged.

Behind him, on each side of the sash window, hung coloured elevations of a house and a bungalow, but on none of the walls hung the professional certificate of a man who'd entered the business regularly.

Not that Cheyne-Chevington wouldn't have certificates . . . only they weren't to do with selling property!

'Any comment?'

Hastings shrugged. 'Go ahead. Think what you like.'

'Right. I think you're Cheyne-Chevington. And I'm going to ask you some other questions.

'What dealings have you had with Hugh Groton?'

'Who says I've had any dealings with him?'

'A person of your description was seen at his farm a short time before the tiger escaped. This man inspected the tiger and its cage, then sat in Groton's car talking to him. Groton parks his vehicles in the same shed and the man may also have inspected Groton's truck.'

'I don't buy tigers or trucks.'

'Were you that man?'

'I was not.'

'But you know Groton.'

'I've seen him around.'

'But do you know him?'

'I've . . . drunk in his presence.'

'Where – how often?'

'How the devil should I know? There's one or two bars that everyone uses, the Angel, the Two Flags, places like that. I've never had more than a couple of words with him.'

'A couple of words about Shimpling?'

'Why should I talk to him about Shimpling?'

'It was a subject you had in common. Shimpling was in Kenya along with Groton.'

'No! I've never talked to him about Shimpling.'

'Where were you on the night of August twelfth last year?'

Hastings picked up a glass paperweight from the desk and began cupping it from one hand to the other. The mouth was tight. He was sitting forward, eyes lowered to the shuttling weight.

But if he'd really been a respectable property agent, would he have been submitting to this inquisition?

'I know very well where I was on the night of August twelfth last year.'

'Good. You seem to have an excellent memory for some things.'

'You know what you can do with your sarcasm! I have an excellent reason for remembering. I spent that weekend with Ted Cockfield at his place in Weston-le-Willows.'

'Who's Ted Cockfield?'

'Don't you know?'

Perkins said: 'He's a building contractor. He's got a big yard near the station ... has a river chalet at Weston-le-Willows.

'He's also an alderman,' Hastings said. 'An ex-mayor, a family man, a well-known contributor to charities. Good enough?'

'Who else was there?'

'Another fellow. It was a stag party. Mrs Ted was at Torquay with their son Tommy and his wife.'

'Were there servants at the chalet?'

'There was the daily who keeps it squared-up. It's only a glorified bungalow that Ted uses at weekends. We went down there on the Friday night and didn't come back till midday Monday. Ted keeps a yacht there. We did some sailing. I never heard about the tiger till the Sunday papers.'

'What was the name of the other fellow?'

'I don't remember—'

'What was his name?'

'Ken. Ken Ashfield.' Hastings clutched the paper-weight convulsively. 'He's a chemist – ask your pal there – he keeps the shop in Abbeygate.'

'Another alderman?'

'What's that got to do with it? He's a member of the Athenaeum.'

'And the daily?'

'What about the daily?'

76

'Doesn't she have similar claims to credibility?'

Hastings scowled at him – precisely the scowl of the photograph lying on the desk. Beard, moustache, a different hair-parting, they were suddenly and obviously mere props.

'I seem to have heard all this before,' Gently said. 'Groton also has an unimpeachable alibi. They seem to grow wild in these parts – it was only the tiger who didn't have one. What time did you leave here on the Friday?'

'How should I know? After business.'

'Before six?'

'Before six! Nearer half past four, I should say.'

'How many cars?'

'My Jag. We picked up Ted from one of his sites.'

'Go on.'

'Then we drove down to Weston and had a meal at the Red Lion. After that, to the chalet. We played rummy. I won a bit. We killed a bottle of whisky and went to bed pretty high.'

'Who was high?'

'We all were.'

'Not just Cockfield and the chemist?'

'All of us, I'm telling you! We went to bed after midnight.'

'In separate rooms?'

'Separate rooms.'

'So you could have gone out with nobody knowing?'

Hastings slammed the paperweight on the desk. 'Yes! I could have gone out a dozen times – except that

I was too sozzled to get the car out – and they'd have heard me doing it, anyway!

'The garage is bung under the bedrooms and the driveway is new gravel – and, anyway, Cockfield has a dog.

'That's that – I didn't go out!'

'How long have you known these two men?'

Hastings gave his head a despairing lift. 'Since I joined the Athenaeum. Over two years ago.'

'Who put you up?'

'Sam Sayers.'

'The man who used to have this business?'

'Yes.'

'I'd like to talk to him.'

Hastings paused, then said: 'Well, you won't talk to him in Abbotsham.

'He's retired, you understand? That's why he sold me the business. He lived upstairs in the flat till last September, then he went off to Bournemouth. He left a forwarding address but—'

'Now you don't have it by you!'

'Why should I? He had no relatives. Nothing came for him but pamphlets . . .'

What was extraordinary was the note of self-justification in Hastings's voice, as though in some way he felt himself responsible because Sayers had no relatives.

'Anyway, I've lost the address – it was some hotel or guest house – and nothing's come for him since Christmas. If you want him you'll have to look for him.'

'I see.'

But where had that note of self-justification come from?

Hastings was mauling the paperweight again, shuffling it back and forth on the desk.

'He left in September . . . not August?'

'September. I can't remember the date.'

'Taking his furniture?'

'I bought it off him. I live in the flat now.'

'I wonder what his alibi would have been for the night of August twelfth last year.'

Hastings stammered: 'What's the use of looking at me?'

Gently shook his head. Then he rose to go.

CHAPTER SEVEN

DUTT, WHO HADN'T followed them up the stairs, joined them again in the Buttermarket, a pleased complacency showing on his chunky face.

'Thought I'd go out for a cuppa, chief . . .'

He pointed to a Lyons across the street. It was plumb opposite Hastings's office and about forty yards distant.

Gently grunted. 'What have you got?'

'Well . . . I chatted the bird at the counter first. But she'll have a crush on her boss, I couldn't get anything out of her. So I went across the road. The cafeteria's on the first floor. You can sit at a table by the window and watch all that goes on over the street.'

'What did you see?'

'First, I palled up with a waitress, one who looked as though she'd been there for a while. Told her I'd been to see David Hastings, and that I'd heard he was a one for the girlies. Yes, she said, he was that all right, he'd had some smart pieces up there. Quite a scandal it was with the waitresses, it put the young ones off their work.

'Was he steady with anyone? I asked. Yes, she said, he'd got a blonde. Very well dressed, drives a blue Merc, been regular with him for quite a time. Usually turns up after the office closes, but they've seen them hugging in the upstairs office.'

'A blonde, eh . . . ?'

'So she says. Shirley Banks is a blonde, chief.'

'She'd have to have risen a bit in the world to fit the rest of the description. Anyone you know, Inspector?'

Perkins shook his head disconsolately.

'I hope they serve good cuppas here,' Gently said. 'We may need a man up there, drinking them. What else, Dutt?'

'As soon as you went out, chief, Hastings grabbed up the phone and dialled a number. And he wasn't ringing the bird downstairs, because she kept banging away at a typewriter.'

'Ringing his pals,' Gently said, 'to let them know we'd be round checking.'

'Or ringing the blonde,' Dutt said, 'to warn her off from coming here.'

Gently shrugged. 'We might not be interested. Could be it's nothing to do with us. But a blonde is a blonde is a blonde . . . perhaps you'd better go back and have tea there, Dutt.'

'That's the way I feel about it, chief.'

'Also, you can keep an eye on Hastings.'

Dutt went.

Perkins said: 'That's Cheyne-Chevington all right, isn't it?' Gently nodded. 'Not much doubt. But we'll have to pin him down on that. Put a man on checking – tax office, National Insurance, licence office – and borrow specimens of his handwriting. We'll get witnesses who can identify him if neceessary.'

'I knew I'd seen the man in that photograph.'

'Do you remember a blonde from when he lived near you?'

'I'll ask the wife. She may remember. What do you think – is he the chummie?'

Gently smiled at the eager local man, began to walk back towards Headquarters. How could it possibly be a coincidence that Cheyne-Chevington was on the spot? And yet . . .

'I don't think we'll find he's the one who drove the truck. We'll check his alibi, of course. But I imagine it will stand up.'

'But if he went to arrange about the tiger . . . !'

'We're only guessing it was him. I think it was, but it doesn't follow he was the chummie in the job.

'Look at the pattern. Groton has the tiger, so he's out – he must have an alibi. Cheyne-Chevington sets it up, but he's vulnerable too – another alibi.

'What we're looking for is a third man, one who has no traceable connection with Shimpling – a man who *doesn't* need an alibi, because we wouldn't think to check it. Also, if this third man's alone in the world and can vanish after the job's done . . . that's perfect!

'The link is missing, and we can never bring it home to them.'

'And the third man . . . ?'

'Samuel Sayers. It seems to stick out a mile.'

'But Sayers . . .'

'Did you know him?'

'Yes. I found him a likeable sort of chap.'

'That's not the point! Tell me about him. How old was he, for a start?'

'Oh, he wasn't so very old – mid-fifties, I'd say; medium height, podgy build, gone bald on top.'

'Pretty active?'

'Oh yes. He used to be secretary of the Lads' Club. Went in for badminton and judo – he could send you sailing over his shoulder. But all the same . . .'

'He fits the bill. I'd say he was just the man we were looking for. Especially his being a judo expert – he'd probably have needed to lay Shimpling out.'

'But I rather liked him.'

Gently grinned. 'We'll have to dig him up,' he said. 'We can start by phoning a description to Bournemouth, though Hastings may have given us that for a blind. Then we can try the post office and the banks . . . perhaps his bank'll be the best bet.

'Where a man's account is transferred to isn't confidential information.'

'I don't know . . .' Perkins said, wriggling.

'Remember, the fellow was a queer.'

Perkins's ears reddened about the lobes. He muttered:

'That lot happened before I knew him . . .'

They talked on, along Abbeygate Street, filled now with rush-hour traffic. Above ornate, bronze-framed windows a gilded glass panel read: K. Ashfield, MPS.

Gently tried the door, but it was locked, and a card

83

said: 'Closed Even for Larner's Liver Pills'. Inside the shop looked cool and tidy. Gently hunched his shoulders. Tomorrow . . .

'One other thing to bear in mind.'

They were crossing Abbey Plain and could see two reporters.

'The "black book" – in the last analysis, that may be the key to this business. We've already a "G" and an "H" and an "S', and now an "A" and a "C" from Ashfield and Cockfield. Of course, it needn't mean a thing – but the right initials keep turning up.

'Give us just one or two more, and it'll have to stop being a coincidence.'

Perkins's unhappy eyes turned on him.

'You can't mean you suspect Alderman Cockfield!'

'Shsh,' Gently said.

The two reporters were on them.

'How's it going, Super?'

Work, it seemed, was over for the day. In Bradfield's office the chief constable was waiting to sweep Gently off home with him.

His name was Villiers and he had a twist in his nose as though it had once been broken and badly set; also his chin stuck out sharply. Yet he was handsome, in his rough-hewn way.

'Bradfield's been telling me you've spotted your man – a struck-off medico, isn't he? Hastings, the fellow who took over Sam Sayers's. You never can tell in this game, I say . . .'

An ex-army man, as like as not. He probably got that

84

nose boxing. He had a hard, over-riding voice with a touch of Bow Bells in its accent.

No doubt a bastard if you rubbed him the wrong way, and that wouldn't be difficult. He'd have favourites . . .

'Not local, of course, that fellow. I meet him on club nights. Don't like him. Bit of a pansy with that beard, eh . . . easy to spot them. I'm not surprised.'

'You've reason to think he's a homosexual?'

'What? No – nothing of that kind! I mean the way he dresses . . . his manner. If I'd known him better I'd have black-balled him.'

'Was Groton ever put up for the Athenaeum?'

'No, but I like him. He's a bit of a card.'

Soon it was evident enough how Villiers had spent his afternoon. He'd been collecting the local notables to meet Gently at dinner.

'Nothing formal, y'know . . . just a meal with friends . . . the Mayor and one or two others.'

Did it really matter who murdered Shimpling?

They drove to Villiers's house in Villiers's Bentley. The house was out of town. Villiers drove fast and well. When they arrived three other cars were already parked on the sweep and through French windows came the sound of laughter and a chink of glasses.

'You'd like to join them in a drink?'

Gently would rather have had a cup of tea, but soon he had a Scotch grasped in his left hand while he was shaking hands with his right.

'Alderman Parkins, our present Mayor . . .'

A faded, ascetic-looking man.

'Geoffrey Traynor . . .'

Of Traynor's Fine Ales.

'And here's the missus, dying to meet you . . .'

And the Chairman of the Bench of Magistrates, the town clerk and the fire chief, all flushed and being familiar and making jokes and shooting questions.

Well, they could have their fun. In another twenty-four hours . . .

But just now his head was swimming and he wished he was safe in the Angel, reading *Pickwick*.

The room, in spite of open French windows, had the suffocating airlessness that went with the absence of a fireplace.

'Alderman Cockfield . . .'

Cockfield? Now he was alert again!

A powerful, moon-faced man with thinned grey hair, who stared and shook hands challengingly.

'How do, Superintendent. What do you think of our little job?'

In his late fifties. The hands, the body of a man who'd worked his way up from the bottom.

'Nothing special from your point of view, but it makes a stir here in Abbotsham. Not that the fellow was worth making a fuss about. I read in the paper he was a blackmailer.'

'Does that make a difference?'

'It would for me, I can tell you. I hate blackmailers. So far as I'm concerned, this Shimpling got what was coming to him.'

'What do you recommend us to do, then?'

'What? You'll have to do your duty, won't you? A

man must always do that, whether he likes it or not. Do your duty. But don't do a stroke more than that.

'Work to rule – that's the ticket! We shan't mind if you don't find the fellow.'

'Old Ted is a Socialist,' Villiers chipped in.

'Labour, Bill – I'm not ashamed of it. I'm the biggest employer in Abbotsham – and the biggest red. Ask anyone.'

'He'll talk Marx to you.'

'And why not? I'll talk Marx to any intelligent man . . .'

And there he was, setting his drink down, as though about to strip and roll up his sleeves.

But out of the corner of his eye he was watching Gently, playing to him, watching the effect . . .

'I've been talking to David Hastings.'

At once he had Cockfield's attention.

'Hastings? He's all right, Hastings.'

Villiers stood by anxiously, nursing his glass.

'You're friendly with him?'

'Oh, I don't know. So-so. See him around.'

'Do you often invite him to your chalet at Weston?'

'Didn't know – oh yes! He was there once.'

'When was that?'

Cockfield hoisted his shoulders like a comic Jewish gentleman.

'Why you ask me that, huh? Why not ask Dave Hastings?' Gently matched the shrug.

'It doesn't matter. It wouldn't be the weekend when the tiger escaped.'

Cockfield stared. 'He says it wasn't?'

'What do you say, Mr Cockfield?'

Cockfield didn't say anything for a moment, then he burst into loud laughter.

'He knows his business, this one, Bill! No use trying to sell him short. And it's Old Ted, Mr Superintendent – Ted the Red. Bottoms up!'

A moment later a gong began to sound and Mrs Villiers signalled her husband.

During the meal Gently had Cockfield seated on his left. The big contractor talked ceaselessly, cramming food into his mouth as he did so.

He drank wine as though it were beer, swigging down glassfuls in single gulps; then he'd help himself from the bottle and top up Gently's glass at the same time.

'Skaal, Super!'

He grew merry, yet one could swear it was half put on.

Round the table they exchanged glances. Old Ted was on form tonight!

'D'you think they could use me in Westminster, Super? I'd be a stumbling-block for them, what? A Labour backbencher with seven hundred employees . . . never a strike in twenty years.

'You want to know why? They can talk to me! We use the same sort of language. I'll sit on a plank and roll a fag and quote them Lenin by the shovelful . . .

'Skaal!

'I'm not a boss, I'm a leader, Super . . .'

While, down his temples, sweat rolled in streams, so that he had to break off to dab with his handkerchief.

Across the table, the ascetic-looking Parkins was eating nut-meat and salad. He was short-sighted and kept squinting at Cockfield as though one of Groton's animals were sitting opposite him.

On Gently's right, the Chairman of the Bench tried to begin a legal anecdote; but he was too studied and long-winded to make any headway against Cockfield.

'Skaal! You're not drinking, Super. Try some of this . . . what is it? Chablis! I don't know one wine from another, that's a job for the wine merchant . . .

'Look, you're an intelligent man, Super, you're a man I can talk to. Nationalization is bunk – I'll prove it to you. It's like this.'

'Spare us Nationalization!' someone called.

No,' Cockfield said. 'No. I know you rabble don't care a hoot – but the Super, he's different!

'Nationalization – what is it? It's trying to force a natural process. We'll get it, anyway, that's my point – it's an economic inevitability.

'Take the chemical industry – two big cartels, trying to do each other down – one'll swallow the other, then what? The last takeover – by the Bank! That's Nationalization as a natural process, a historic process.

'Skaal!'

But now he was getting a little fuddled, because he spilled the wine down his shirt front.

'Mr Cockfield is a character,' the chairman murmured. 'He made an excellent Mayor, though . . . which reminds me . . . ?'

'When was he Mayor?' Gently asked.

'He held office last year, before Mr Parkins.'

Parkins heard his name mentioned and squinted severely. He drank a little water from a tumbler.

'Mr P. is a hotelier,' the chairman murmured. 'Which reminds me . . .'

'Skaal!'

By the end of the meal there was no doubt that Cockfield was squiffy. He had to be assisted into the lounge, and Villiers helped him drink his coffee.

But still he wanted to sit by Gently, still he kept his eye on him, while he rambled on about politics and whatever came into his head.

He'd really taken to Gently! The others couldn't get a look in. Villiers was mooning around the two of them like an unhappy hen who'd hatched ducklings.

'I want to see you tomorrow, Super . . . show you round . . . what about it?'

'Too busy.'

'Don't be like that, man! Who cares a damn about . . . what's his name?'

'Shimpling.

'That's him! Well . . . who cares about him? He's dead, best thing too . . . I want to show you my sites.'

'I'll see.'

'That's better. Y'know, I like you, Superintendent . . . who's driving you back?'

'Mr Villiers.'

'Just put me in the car . . . you'll find I can drive!'

But actually it was Parkins, stone sober, who drove them back in his Daimler, with Gently supporting the snoring Cockfield as they proceeded at a sedate forty.

They dropped Cockfield off at a large house on the

outskirts of the town, where he was taken in by his son Tommy, who showed no surprise.

As they drove away, Parkins said:

'That fellow killed a man, you know.'

Adding, as Gently turned to him:

'It should have been manslaughter, but of course it passed off as careless driving.'

'When was this?'

'When he was in office. Last May twelvemonth, I think. Ask Villiers.'

'Thanks, I will.'

Parkins went on driving, chin high.

CHAPTER EIGHT

I N THE LOUNGE of the Angel Dutt sat alone, reading the marked copy of *Pickwick*. It was a thick, early edition with the plates, and Dutt was frowning at it through his reading glasses. When Gently entered he put it down.

'Hello, chief. Have a good evening?'

Gently grimaced and took a chair. He closed his eyes and leaned backwards.

'I've been having a go at this Dickens bloke . . . they must have been a rum lot in his day! I reckon he overwrote, you know. Blinking great paragraphs and long sentences.'

'It went down big when he wrote it.'

'Perhaps we've got on a bit since those days. I don't know, but I'm not with it. I reckon he did things the hard way,'

'What did you have for tea?'

'Bangers and chips with an egg.'

'Any good?'

'So-so. Bangers don't vary much, chief.'

Gently opened his eyes slightly.

'All right,' he said. 'What's her name?'

'Lady Buxhall.'

'Who?'

'Lady Buxhall. Lord Buxhall's missus.'

Gently opened his eyes wide, then closed them again.

'Nuts,' he said. 'You've delusions of grandeur. Keep *Debrett* out of this one, Dutt.'

'But it's right, chief!'

'Nuts.'

'I've got her description and the lot. Lady Laura Betty Buxhall, née Potter. Used to be a model for Burns and Winsmoore.'

'A model, was she?' Gently opened one eye.

'That's how old Buxhall picked her up. Before that she might have been something else — someone who had dealings with Cheyne-Chevington.'

Gently nodded. 'Go on,' he said. 'Though I think you're ten jumps ahead. But let's go back to the bangers and chips and what the policeman saw through the window.'

'I saw her, chief. No doubt about it. Tall. Ash blonde. Lean build. Driving a light blue Mercedes coupé, licence number B22.

'I called the waitress over and she confirmed it was the same blonde. This was about ten minutes to six. She was only there a quarter of an hour.'

'Snogging with Hastings.'

'Not snogging. They were talking nineteen to the dozen. Hastings was walking up and down. She was

93

smoking a fag in a long holder. Then before she left he did kiss her, but they didn't make a ball of it. She came out looking rather peevish. He went up into the flat and poured himself a drink.'

'Then, naturally, you did some research.'

'What do you think, chief? The car belongs to Lady Buxhall and the blonde answers her description. The Buxhalls live at Hawley House, about twenty miles from Abbotsham. That's near Illingford, in the next county, which is perhaps why people don't know her up this way.

'Then I rang the *Express* Building and talked to Stan Taylor, the gossip columnist. She's Buxhall's second. He's pushing seventy and is reckoned to be worth over a million.

'He has a son and two daughters who are daggers drawn with Lady Laura, but the old man is besotted with her, so they've had their noses put out of joint.

'He met her at a party at Claridges where Burns and Winsmoore put on a show. There was a whirlwind romance. He married her about four years ago. She's behaved like a model wife, and Taylor says she better had, because if the family catch her slipping it'll be lights for Lady Laura.

'That's the lot, chief. She doesn't have form. Thought I'd wait up and give it to you.'

'Hmm,' Gently said.

He took out a card on which he'd pencilled the 'black book' initials. He put a tick against the 'B'.

Six out of ten . . . four to go!

Enough to rule out coincidence? Now it began to

look that way. And here was enough money involved to motivate half a dozen murders . . .

'She'd be a wide-open touch for Shimpling.'

'She'd come to hand like a pint pot, chief. If he was keeping tabs on Hastings he'd soon find out about her. Was she in the book for much?'

'"B" was paying fifty a month.'

'I'd say that was a pretty reasonable touch.'

'Shimpling was fly. He was a clever operator.'

Dutt tucked his head on one side. 'I reckon this is the angle, chief,' he said. 'This is where the big money is, where Shimpling might have stepped out of line. There's Lady Laura, sweating on a million, and Hastings sweating on it with her – and all of it ready to go up the spout at a couple of words from Shimpling.

'And that fifty a month was only going to last till Lord Buxhall turned it in.

'I'd say Shimpling tried for a lump sum and got the tiger set on him instead.'

'Yes, the tiger . . .'

Gently fetched out his pipe and began sucking it, cold. That improbable tiger! And after the tiger, even more inexplicable happenings at the bungalow.

For if the idea of using the tiger had been to make the murder appear an accident, why had someone then buried the body, and locked the door – and stolen the car?

Of course, the car theft may have been unconnected . . . but that was the least of the improbable features.

'Let's try it for size,' he said. 'Granted that Shimpling had got too greedy. So there's a plot between Hastings and Lady Laura to put Shimpling away. What gave them the idea of using the tiger? It's too bizarre, almost inconceivable. Only one person would even dream of it, and that's a person who owned a tiger.'

'Groton.'

'Groton. And what follows? Groton must have been in the plot. He must have been known to Hastings and Lady Laura as another Shimpling victim. But how? Blackmailers are usually careful to keep their victims from knowing each other, and here we have a combination too unlikely to have been mere chance.

'You don't say to a stranger in a pub, "I'm being blackmailed – what about you?"!'

'Shimpling may have let something out, chief.'

'He's never shown up as a careless type. But, however it was, this is what we're faced with – Groton was in it with the other two.

'So the plot is laid. Groton is out. He must have an alibi above suspicion. Hastings too – he's involved with Shimpling: inquiry would reveal his true identity. Groton's alibi is easy, but Hastings has to cast about him. He chooses a weekend in the country with an ex-mayor and a respectable chemist.

'But here there's mystery again – these two men have "black book" initials; and I've just learned that Cockfield may have had a handle for Shimpling to use. Two more possible victims who were known to the others, and in the plot! It begins to look as though Shimpling's clients were ganging up to put him away.'

'Then Hastings's alibi is a fake?'

'We have to take that into consideration. Let's say

for the moment it's by no means innocent. But the same goes for the others, if we can pin them down as Shimpling victims – Hastings, Cockfield and Ashfield, they're equally in it or out of it.

'We'll suppose they're out of it. Hastings was vulnerable, and the job of the other two would be to give him cover. But there was another man who wasn't vulnerable and we'll presume it was he who did the job.

'Samuel Sayers, the man who sold the estate business to Hastings. He vanished from Abbotsham after the tiger scare and Hastings doesn't want us to find him. He was a queer, which would be his handle as far as Shimpling was concerned. He lived in the flat over the office and he has a "black book" initial.

'This is what may have happened. Groton left the tiger loaded. Sayers collected it and drove to the bungalow and parked the truck at a distance from it.

'He knocked at the door. He was a judo expert. He laid Shimpling out cold. Then he backed the truck up to the door and raised the grille and released the tiger.

'After that we can only assume he left the tiger to get on with his meal, then came back later to search the place and to remove the blackmail evidence.

'Which should have been all – but for some reason it wasn't all. Sayers, or somebody, buried the body, locked the door and stole the car.

'Unless an outsider got into the act, what happened afterwards doesn't make sense.'

Gently yawned and look at Dutt.

'Your pigeon, Inspector,' he said.

Dutt riffled the pages of the marked Pickwick, made the wrinkles show round his eyes.

'Sounds a bit circumstantial, chief,' he said. 'There's a lot of supposing goes with it.'

'I'm glad you noticed that.'

'But I reckon it could have worked out that way. All we need is a bit of routine, just to fill in the blank spaces.'

'How's it going to fill in what happened at the bungalow?'

'Well . . . suppose chummie was scared of the tiger . . .'

'Go on.'

'I wouldn't have liked to have gone back there . . . not knowing if the tiger was around or not. So suppose he didn't go back till the next night. Then he gets the seconds and buries the body . . . then maybe the second time he comes on foot, and pinches the car to make his getaway.'

'This case will make you or break you, Dutt.'

'But couldn't it have happened that way, chief . . . ?'

'No it couldn't. Shimpling had tradesmen delivering. The door was locked before they arrived.'

Yet who indeed would have had the courage to return to the bungalow that night, inviting, at every step, the terrible fate which had happened to Shimpling – and with the horrible spectacle of that fate fresh and uppermost in his mind?

It needed another 'cat-man', another Groton.

But Groton had a Bank of England alibi . . .

Was it possible that in the case was another skilled cat-handler?

'Really, we don't seem to have very much, chief.'

Gently sighed, nodded.

'When it comes to facts . . . I mean what you can prove. We're sort of just left holding the tiger.'

'Better sleep on it, Dutt.'

'Yes, chief. I will.'

'Perhaps they'll turn up Banks or Sayers.'

'Yes, chief.'

Perhaps! But he felt vaguely aggrieved that he had nothing better to offer his assistant.

On the surface, he had given the case outline, but it was pretty thin stuff underneath. Unless he could get his teeth in tomorrow he wasn't going to leave Dutt with much to make bricks from.

Somebody else had come into the lounge, Harry Barnes, the Smith's PA man. He stood nursing a whisky glass at a discreet distance, but obviously waiting to catch Gently's eye. Now he caught it and came over.

'Any stop-press, chiefie . . . ?'

'Are you a resident?'

Barnes grinned and nodded and waved his glass.

'If Dickens could sleep here, why not me? I've got a shake-down in the billiards room. Thought I'd stick close to the fountain-head in case I came in for a special issue.'

'I've nothing for you.'

Even his old friends of the Press he was letting down.

'Oh well . . . it would miss the countries. And, anyway, I've something else to tell you.'

99

He sat down, a dumpy man who would never look anything but untidy, for whom factories turned out baggy brown suits and shoes with uppers that always cracked. But he had bright and friendly eyes.

'The boys got a rush of blood this afternoon. They had a hunch that Groton's the man and they all drove out there to give him the treatment.'

'Did he offer them tea?'

'Pull the other one. He let fly with a twelve-bore.'

'Did he now?'

'Both barrels, and he had another gun ready loaded.'

Gently grinned to himself. 'What are you going to do – sue him?'

'You know us better than that, chiefie. It'll make every front page tomorrow morning. And it'll be slanted, you know. The readers will guess what we're guessing. Mind you, he fired the shot wide, but we could hear the pellets whistle over.'

'Well, it's too early for pheasants. Perhaps he took you for grouse.'

'Come off it, chiefie! It's serious, isn't it? He could just as easily have peppered one of us.'

'What happened then?'

'Big reversings! No room to turn in that lane. We drew off out of range and held a committee meeting about it. Some of them wanted to creep up on him.'

'But nobody did.'

'Nobody did. Instead we collared his two farmhands when they knocked off at half-five.'

'Any luck?'

'Only background stuff. One of them told us how

he wrestled a bear. He throttled the bear till it was senseless, then just dumped it in the truck.

'Still, the boys weren't satisfied, and they left a couple there to keep watch. But nothing happened except Groton took off and was last seen heading for London.'

'. . . London?'

'Well, the London Road. He drove through here and kept going.'

Gently hesitated. 'When was this?'

'Around seven p.m . . . is there something in it?'

'Would he know you fellows were watching him?'

'Shouldn't think so . . . what's the score, chiefie?'

Gently shook his head. No score at all! Groton could drive to London if he wanted. He had connections there, like the Safari Club, and probably a number of business contacts. His animals, for instance, would be shipped there . . .

Why did Gently feel suddenly alerted?

'What was he driving?'

'Probably his estate car. The boys would have said if he was in the truck.'

'Finish your drink.'

'Do you think he's skipping?'

'I don't think anything you can print.'

He got up, went into the hall. There was still a light in the office. He tapped. The manager answered the door. Over the manager's shoulder peered the pretty face of the receptionist.

'Sorry to interrupt! Have you a London directory?'

'Oh . . . the directory! Yes, Superintendent.'

'I'd like to use your phone.'

They came out, the girl smoothing her skirt. Gently went in and closed the door. He found the Safari Club Number and put through a call.

'Chief Superintendent Gently, CID. I'm trying to contact one of your members.'

'Which one, sir?'

'Hugh Groton. Has he booked for tonight?'

'Just a minute, sir.'

Two minutes passed, then:

'No sir, he's not here. I can give you his home number . . .'

'Don't bother,' Gently grunted.

But then, to check, he did ring the farm, and listened to the ringing tone buzzing hollowly.

Groton wasn't in . . . what then? He might be burying his troubles with a blonde in town!

Out in the hall the manager was all smiles, but the receptionist wore an indignant expression. In the lounge Harry Barnes was trying to pump Dutt, who could scarcely keep his eyes open, and was answering in monosyllables.

CHAPTER NINE

'CHARLES DICKENS SLEPT here': it was painted over the door of his room. In the morning, Gently was inclined to add: 'And George Gently Didn't'.

But it wasn't the room's fault. Though it resembled a corner of a well-kept folk museum, it was spacious and quiet, and the bed was comfortable, and the bedlinen smelled of hot irons.

To look about it, you would suppose Dickens had spent his working life there. Attributed to him were a davenport, a desk chair, a silver inkstand, a sheaf of pens, a backscratcher, a warming-pan and some embroidered slippers in a glass case.

Also the bed, a mahogany four-poster (though now supplied with a spring mattress), which had embroidered damask curtains and canopy, prudently protected with nylon net.

Over the marble mantelpiece hung a print of the author in a double-Hogarth frame, and on the walls Phiz illustrations depicting the history of Mr Pickwick.

A little overpowering, perhaps, to the casual

bed–and–breakfast guest – but not the reason why Gently was sleepless, and woke from a nap with pounding temples.

Breakfast, too, was rather trying.

'Fruit juice, black coffee and two aspirins.'

'There's a very nice mixed grill this morning, sir . . .'

'Just what I said! . . . make it three aspirins.'

And he sipped and frowned and watched Dutt eating his mixed grill with absorbed relish. The devil take Abbotsham and its lionizing! After this, draught bitter.

He wanted to be out in the air, but when he got there things were no better. It was the same sort of sultry, light-overcast day which he had sweated through yesterday. Abbotsham weather! As though the district lay in an airless pocket of its own. As though the sea breezes, not far distant, were turned aside from these somnolent streets.

To make matters worse, it was Saturday market. You could hardly shove your way along the pavements. Cattle-floats, exuding farmyard odours, stood jammed in the traffic, their occupants lowing.

At the junction of the Buttermarket was wedged a horse-drawn lorry decorated in the colours of Abbotsham FC. Today was the opening match of the season, a local derby which was a crowd-puller. Already some morons with their rattles . . .

'Wish I was at White Hart Lane today, chief.'

Then, as they were just turning into Headquarters, an oaf on the car park set off a cracker.

'Don't you bother with by-laws in these parts?'

A constable they met at the door was flabbergasted.

He tried, and failed, to click his heels, then aimed a salute and hastily made off. Perkins, who'd opened his door at that moment, stared round-eyed dismay at the belligerent Yard man.

'They've been on the phone . . .'

'I should jolly well hope so!'

'They've found Shimpling's car . . .'

'Don't shout at me!'

He sat down at Perkins's desk and ran a hand over his forehead. How many drinks had it been last night? At least he hadn't kept pace with Cockfield.

Perkins wavered in front of him.

'A man named Smalley has got it, Super . . .'

'Got what?'

'Shimpling's car, Super.'

'Oh. Where did he get it?'

'He bought it from a dealer in Fulham. Peckthorne's Garage, Craven Archways. Smalley lives in Fulham himself, he's a rep for Bignall's Potted Meats . . .'

'I don't want to know about potted meats!'

'Pardon, Super?'

'Where did this garage get hold of the car?'

'Oh, the chummie who sold it pretended he was Shimpling. It was a legal sale as far as they know.'

'Did he give an address?'

'Only a false one . . .'

'Do the garage remember him?'

'No, Super.'

'When did they buy the car?'

'September seventh last year.'

'And a fat lot of good all that's going to do us!'

Perkins couldn't make it out. His cod's-eyes pop-ped, he gaped at Gently. He glaced at Dutt. The placid Londoner was quietly rolling a cigarette.

'Well, at least we know, Super . . .'

'We don't know anything. Who's checking the banks for Sayers's account?'

'Sergeant Hargrave . . .'

'Now tell me something. Wasn't Alderman Cock-field pinched last year?'

Worse and worse! Perkins wobbled, found a chair, sat down. In this same office he'd made subordinates tremble, but now he'd have given his leave to be out of it. Twice he tried to begin to say something.

'Well?'

'It was only a small matter, Super . . .'

'He killed a man?'

'No . . . yes! It was an accident . . . he must have swerved . . . he hit a young fellow on a scooter.'

'When was this?'

'After Christmas – the year before last, that is! As a rule he's a good driver. Never had his licence endorsed.'

'Were there any witnesses?'

'No . . . it was late. He reported the accident himself.'

'So I should think. Was he loaded?'

Perkins squirmed. 'No – of course!'

'Otherwise it would have been manslaughter.'

Gently nodded to himself, winced, stopped.

'Look here, Inspector, I want the truth of this! The official version isn't good enough. I think Cockfield was being blackmailed, and this little affair could have been the occasion of it.

'Frankly now – what are the facts?'

'He was fined, Super . . .'

'But he might have been jugged!'

Perkins wriggled about on his chair, his face the colour of stewed raspberries. Was it fair to ask him this? Surely Gently could have gone higher?

But there he sat, at Perkins's own desk, his eyes biting into the local man. . .

Perkins gulped.

'It was around eleven . . . he was driving home down Nelson Street . . . the youngster, his name was Cliff Amies, he'd been visiting his girl at Hartshill. Cockfield swerved on to his wrong side, hit Amies, killed him. He went on driving home, rang us up when he got there.'

'How long afterwards?'

'Well . . . an hour.'

'Who took his statement?'

'I went out.'

'Was he canned?'

'He was when I got there . . . slipping down whiskies, one after another.'

'So like that you couldn't give him a test.'

'There wasn't much point in it, was there?'

'None at all. If he claimed he'd been sober you'd have to take his word . . . which, of course, you did.'

Perkins squirmed but said nothing.

'Go on. What was the statement?'

'He said the light on the scooter dazzled him . . . we checked the lamp, it was focused high.'

'Where had Cockfield come from?'

'He said from the cinema . . . we had to take his word there. After the accident he didn't know what he was doing, that's why he drove on without stopping.'

'So – a wigging, a fine, a suspension – instead of maybe three years!'

'We did check . . .'

'But not too hard . . . not on a mayor during his term of office.'

Gently smoothed his throbbing head again. There it was, a Shimpling set-up. If Cockfield had been drinking before the accident, and Shimpling knew it, Shimpling was in. Even if he'd guessed that Cockfield was high he might have found ways to put the screw on . . .

'Were there any postscripts to the business?'

Perkins, scowling at nothing, jerked his head.

'Postscripts . . . ?'

'You know. Perhaps a whisper that there were people who knew more than they'd said.'

'Well yes . . . actually.' Perkins said moistening his lips. 'There was a letter, an anonymous letter – not to us, to the boy's father. Said the writer had evidence that would have altered the verdict – made us a lot of trouble with Amies. He threatened to go to his MP.'

'What does that look like to you?'

'There's always people writing letters like that.'

'To me it looks as though Cockfield were showing sales resistance to Shimpling, and Shimpling put on the screw and brought him to heel. Which means that Cockfield's support for Hastings's alibi is dubious, leaves us with only Ashfield to credit.'

'I just can't believe it of Alderman Cockfield!'

'He's human, isn't he?

'I know . . .'

It was a glimpse of a world, a world different and apart from the metropolis. One where values were static and unrelative, where easy cynicism was out of place.

Where a CID inspector like Perkins could sit blushing like a shamed child, when someone cast aspersion on a Somebody to whom he allotted automatic innocence . . .

And was Gently so superior because he questioned all innocence, all values?

'Anyway, I'll have a talk with this chemist. He may be fireproof though the others aren't.'

'He's a decent fellow,' Perkins blurted eagerly. 'There's never been anything against him.'

'One other thing. I want you to ring Groton and to pitch him a yarn about poachers.'

Perkins was too much bowled out to ponder the ethics of this manoeuvre, though no doubt he would remember and be unhappy about it later. Now he rang Groton, who was at home, and simply repeated what Gently'd told him.

'There was some poaching over your way last night . . . did you hear any shooting around midnight?'

A simple trap – and Groton fell into it.

'Yes . . . I heard shots around half–twelve.'

'Mr Ashfield?'

'He's in the dispensary. I'll ask if he can see you. What name, please?'

She was an austere woman with facial hair and a flat figure. She was one of three, none of them beauties, none of them much under fifty, who were kept busy behind the glass counter, serving the brisk Saturday trade.

When Gently had come in there'd been scarcely standing room in the shop, and he was pushed up against a tall cabinet containing displays of cosmetics.

The air smelled of stale bath salts with whiffs of camphor and more subtle odours, besides a scent of ground coffee proceeding from the basket of one of the shoppers.

For they were country women. Each one of them carried a stuffed bag or basket, seemingly unconscious of the weight, since their burdens were never set down. Yet they dressed well, were apparently affluent. Some of them wore jewellery that wasn't Brummagem. And they were cheerfully paying down crinkled notes for expensive scent, lipsticks, hair-lotions.

At the end of the shop, behind mirror panels, was the cubicle marked DISPENSARY, from which came a shuffle of feet and occasional clinks and now and then the sound of voices.

Two fans turned overhead. The shop furnishings were modern and expensive. The assistants, though dour, were efficient, could identify items sketchily described.

A good business . . .

Shimpling would have noticed, if he'd dropped by for some after-shave lotion.

'This way, sir.'

Was it an accident that the three assistants were such dragons? Policy perhaps; the pretty young ones would come and go too quickly.

This one smelled strongly of menthol lozenges and had a definite tuft on her chin; one of the others had a chopper-like profile, the third a cast in the left eye.

'Mr Ashfield.'

They'd gone through the mirrors into a small, square compartment. Two sides were fitted with benches and a sink and a doorway on the right had stairs descending to it. On shelves above the benches were packed glass bottles, some clear, some dark blue, and the benches were littered with porclain dishes, glass beakers, a mortar and pestle. Made-up prescriptions, each wrapped in white paper, stood neatly grouped on a small desk.

Then there was Ashfield.

'You're a policeman, aren't you?'

He had a high-pitched, whining little voice. He was a small man. He had a perfectly round skull with dark hair oiled and smeared back over it.

'What do you want? I'm rather busy. You must understand this is a busy day.'

He was wearing white overalls but had a spotted bow tie. Because his neck was so short the tie came right up to his chin.

'Mr Kenneth Ashfield?'

'You heard my name.'

'Chief Superintendent Gently, CID. I'm investigating the death of Peter Shimpling. I believe you can help me.'

111

'You can believe what you like, can't you?'

Angry, peppery brown eyes. Darting aggressively at Gently, yet swinging past him all the time. He had rounded cheeks and good straight teeth which appeared triumphantly after each clipped speech.

Or was it perhaps apprehensively . . . since the eyes never backed him up?

'I'd sooner believe the truth, Mr Ashfield. Had you any acquaintance with Shimpling?'

'You don't believe in the truth. Belief is superfluous. You either know something, or you don't know it.'

'I'd like to know if you were acquainted with Shimpling.'

'Truth, too, that's superfluous.'

'That may be—'

'Truth is a lie. A mere intellection, divorced from being.'

'This isn't getting us very far . . .'

'I disagree! I find it stimulating. From your point of view I did know Shimpling, or I didn't know Shimpling. Equally true.'

The toothy smile, a brush from the eyes, then the eyes sliding away. Ashfield was working up a momentum from which it was plain he didn't intend to be diverted.

'Again, from your point of view—'

'Who appoints your assistants?'

'What?'

'Your assistants. They're devilishly plain. One can't admire your taste in women.'

Ashfield was thrown for a moment. His eyes darted about, his smile pulled into a snarl. Then:

112

'That's a case in point, don't you think? Plain is pretty, equally true.'

'But you don't have to engage plain assistants – surely it's unusual in your trade?'

'Unusual and usual—'

'On the cosmetic counter – wouldn't a pretty girl be more the thing? Say a blonde with lots of oomph, that's who you'd expect to find there – a girl who knows how to make up, how to wheedle men into buying presents.

'And how much pleasanter for you – especially when she's here after hours! I'd say you needed a blonde in the shop. Don't tell me you never had one?'

This time Ashfield was really stumped; he went quite still and staring. As though he were trying over words, he made a series of small grunting noises through his nose.

'Yes, a blonde,' Gently said. 'You find them doing this job everywhere . . . good for business, good for the boss! I was quite surprised not to see one here.'

'Look! If this is all you've come for—'

'I didn't come to talk metaphysics.'

'Then exactly why—'

'I thought I made it plain. I want to know if you'd met Shimpling.'

'Why pick on me?'

'Your name was given me.'

'In what connection—!'

Gently shook his head. 'First, I'd like you to answer some questions, then we'll come to the background.'

He heard a step and looked round quickly. A woman

was standing at the foot of the stairs. She was a bold-faced person with grey hair, though her age could not have been more than forty.

She stared at Gently, then at Ashfield. Ashfield flickered his toothy smile. The woman was tall and thick-bodied and dowdily but not inexpensively dressed.

'I'm sorry,' she said. 'I thought you were alone, Kenneth. I'll wait till you're free.'

'I—' Ashfield began.

The woman turned and softly remounted the stairs. Gently winked at Ashfield.

'The missus? he asked.

'What if she is?'

'Nothing . . .'

'Why do you say that?'

But his darting eyes weren't looking at Gently.

CHAPTER TEN

'B UT OF COURSE, you did know Shimpling?'
Ashfield didn't immediately reply. He went across to the desk, opened a small drawer, took out a tablet and swallowed it. Some of the fizz had gone out of him. He stood looking into the open drawer. His oiled hair gleamed metallically under the fluorescents that lit the dispensary.

When he turned, it was to sit down.

'Suppose I did. What then?'

'In what capacity did you know him?'

'As a customer. He bought stuff here.'

'Is that all?'

'I met him out. He used to hang around the bars. He was an interesting talker. Not that I ran into him much.'

'He had a woman living with him.'

'So I've read in the papers.'

'She was a blonde.'

'I've read that too.'

'Didn't you meet her?'

Ashfield burped.

'We can check,' Gently said. 'I just thought you'd maybe save us the trouble. My guess is this woman got a job here. I may be wrong. You can tell me.'

'And . . . if she did?'

'She's very attractive. She's a pro and knows her business. She'd get under any man's skin if she was around for a while. But my guess is she wasn't around long . . . didn't see the week out, perhaps. How long did it take?'

'How long did what take?'

'Getting you in front of a camera.'

Ashfield made his grunting noises, showing his teeth at the floor. Now that his head was tilted forward the bow tie had vanished completely.

'This is your story. I've admitted nothing!'

'But that's how it went, wasn't it? Shimpling took a look at you, weighed the prospects, then attacked the weak spot.

'You've a jealous wife. Don't worry . . . I don't intend to raise my voice! And you, maybe you're a bit starved – keep your wool on, I'm not blaming you! You wouldn't dare to hunt it up, but if it were served on a plate . . . and that's what happened, didn't it? I'll bet she was never out of this dispensary . . .

'Then she'd tell you he was away and that you could come out to the bungalow, perhaps even invent an excuse which would satisfy your wife. But, at a certain point in the proceedings fizzh! off goes a flashbulb – and you're down in the book for twenty-five pounds a month.

'We even know what you paid. Why bother to deny it . . . ?'

Ashfield looked ill. 'For God's sake, stop it! She may be listening on the landing. All right, she's jealous – I give you that . . . couldn't we have talked somewhere else?'

'How did you pass off Shirley Banks?'

'Keep your voice down! I don't admit anything,'

'If there's nothing in it   '

'If there is or not, *she'll* believe it if she hears.'

Gently shrugged. 'I don't want to make trouble for you . . . I'll treat the whole business as confidential. But why not admit it? It's over and done with. Being blackmailed isn't a crime.'

'If I had been blackmailed I'd have gone to the police!'

Gently shook his head. 'Not you. Shimpling was a tradesman when it came to blackmail, he made his way the easy way. What was twenty-five pounds a month? You could lose that comfortably in expenses. It was degrading, no doubt, and you'd liked to have clobbered him, but it was cheap compared with the alternative.

'If there'd been a case, in a town like Abbotsham, how could it ever have been kept from your wife?'

'Not so loud! So if it's over and done with, why do you come raking up muck?'

'Shimpling was murdered.'

'What if he was?'

'You're part of the pattern of that murder.'

Ashfield got up, crept over to the stairs, stood

117

listening several moments. But he would scarcely have heard a movement from that direction above the noises from the shop.

He came back and went to the sink, where he poured himself a glass of water.

A curious, monkeyish little man, with the quick, neat actions of an animal . . .

'You can't drag me into this. It's too absurd. Where's the motive? If I was paying only twenty-five a month, would I have killed a man for that?'

'Who said you killed him?'

'Didn't you?'

'I said you were part of the pattern.'

'What pattern?'

'As I see it, a conspiracy of Shimpling's victims.'

'A conspiracy!' Ashfield gulped water. 'I'd say that's even more absurd! How would they know about each other?'

'Perhaps you can tell me.'

'Well, I can't!'

He was driving himself now, trying to get back on his rails. From the sink, glass in hand, he was giving Gently those explosive glances.

'You don't know anything. You have a theory. You'd like to fit me into your theory. Somebody saw me talking to Shimpling – that's the basis of it, isn't it?'

'Twenty-five pounds.'

'Or twenty! Or thirty! Anyone can make up a figure. Figures are a lie about reality – you don't impress me by quoting figures.'

'Let's quote some facts, then.'

'You don't have any!'

'Here's a small one to go on with. You think you've an alibi for the night of the murder, but you haven't. It's just gone phut.'

'I've . . . it's what?'

'Gone phut. It could have been you set on the tiger.'

'Haven't I told you—'

'Not so loud! You might have drawn the unlucky card.'

'This is crazy!'

He began pacing up and down, still with the glass in his hand. For a short man he had long legs, which gave him a pouncing, bobbing motion. Animal-like . . . was it just possible that Ashfield was the second cat-man? His skull was as round as a Spanish orange, went bobbing, bobbing back and forth.

'Is that what you think? That we got together and sentenced this Shimpling fellow to death – then drew lots as to who should do it – who should play games with a tiger?'

'It makes sense, doesn't it?'

'No!'

'None of you have motive enough separately. But put you together! And with Groton among you, a customer who'd tried these tricks before . . .'

'It wasn't like that!'

'How do you know?'

'I mean, you're wrong all along! Good God, do you think I'd have had anything to do with it – killing anyone – if I'd known?'

'If you'd known what?'

119

'If I'd been mixed up in it – this conspiracy you talk about. What Groton would do is another matter. But me! I wouldn't – I just wouldn't.'

'Yet you were mixed up in it.'

'No!'

'Tell me where you where on the night of the murder.'

'I was out of town, at Weston-le-Willows. With Alderman Cockfield and Dave Hastings.'

'Mixed up in nothing.'

'Haven't I said so?'

'Apart from the giving and getting of alibis.'

'You're crazy if you think—'

'They're both of them in it, and so are you. Those are the facts.'

'No – no!'

The glass was slopping over with the vehemence of Ashfield's denials – yet still he was subduing his voice to little above the level of a whisper. What a woman she must be, the one up the stairs!

A cat-man? Somehow Ashfield wasn't quite fitting the part . . .

'Listen – I can't help what you know about me or anyone else. I had nothing to do with that tiger, nothing to do with Shimpling's death. If it were poison – look at those bottles! You might have suspected me then. I could have dosed his malted milk or slipped a ringer in his vitamin pills.

'I could have done – if I'd wanted to! And wouldn't that have been easier? Would it ever have got to letting loose tigers if I'd been consulted in the matter? It's common sense. I'd nothing to do with it. All the rest doesn't matter.

'I don't have to admit anything – you can see how it was for yourself.'

'Yet someone did set the tiger on Shimpling.'

'Not me! That's the truth.'

'But you can guess.'

'Why should I guess?'

Gently nodded . . . it was a good question!

'At the best, you're sticking your neck out for a charge of accessory after the fact. While if you help us . . .'

'I've admitted nothing.'

'Twenty-five pounds.'

'How will you prove it?'

They were facing each other now, Ashfield with his head tilted upwards. All the pepper had gone out of his eyes; they were suddenly fixed and frank. Then they jumped, slipped sideways. There was some little commotion in the shop. A voice said:

'That's all right, miss – Ken knows me!'

And the door opened. It was Cockfield.

This morning Cockfield was dressed in a bright mixture Irish tweed with a squash hat to match and a canary-coloured waistcoat with medal buttons. He looked surprisingly brisk after his carouse. He had a white carnation in his buttonhole. You'd have taken him for a wealthy farmer who'd brought a herd of bullocks to the stock market. His big face, which the hat suited, shone with cheerfulness and confidence.

'Ah, Superintendent! They told me I'd find you here. I gave them a ring at the station. 'lo, Ken boy – what do you make of him? He's a rum nut, isn't he?'

He laughed loudly, patting Ashfield's arm. Ashfield responded with smiling grunts. Cockfield swept off his hat and tossed it on the desk, knocking two pill-boxes off the pile of prescriptions. He grabbed them up, still chuckling.

'Mustn't muck the goods about! See how neatly he does them up – that's our Ken for you, Super. Are you busy?'

Gently shrugged.

'I'm showing you over some sites, remember? Do you more good than grilling Ken. A fat lot he knows, apart from stinks. What are you after here, anyway?'

'Routine inquiries . . .'

'That's a laugh! You've been giving him a dose of the old Gestapo, I could twig it when I came in.' He winked at Ashfield. 'Don't let him upset you. He's a decent so–and–so when you know him. He and I got drunk last night, he's probably, you know . . . two degrees under.

'Give him one of your special pick-me-ups, the violet muck. That'll fix him.'

He laughed again, went prowling round the dispensary as though to give Ashfield time to follow his suggestion. But Ashfield only stood looking awkward and showing his teeth and grunting. Cockfield stared at the bottles. He was putting on a proper act. He stuck his behind out and his head forward, twiddled his thumbs behind his back.

'What a devil of a lot of junk . . . you'll never use all this stuff, Ken? Enough to lay out half Abbotsham. I'd hate to get in wrong with you.

'AM NIT – what's that?'

'It's a poison.'

'I know, you clot! Why don't you keep a shelf of Scotch? It'd do more good than all your potions . . .'

A proper act: the business executive being jovial with his pals. Bringing an earthy touch of sanity to a situation which had got tense . . .

'See here, Super – NUX VOM. There's a witch's brew for you. You'd vomit pink elephants as well as nuts if you downed a dose of that. What's it for, Ken?'

'Pest control.'

'Say rat poison, brother! Strychnine, isn't it?'

'A form of strychnine.'

'Strychnine's good enough. You wouldn't be fussy if you copped some.'

'There are various forms—'

'Listen to him, Super! Now you know his besetting sin. Conscientiousness, that's it – sometimes he'll drive you up the wall.

'He's a philosopher. Oh, yes! You should hear him lecture on Buddhist philosophy. All about the sound of a glass of water and your face before your parents were born. Drives us mad he does, sometimes, has them arguing till the small hours. And he wouldn't as much as swat a fly.

'I mean it, Super – not a single fly!

'Mr Non-Violence is our Ken. That's not to say he isn't human . . .'

123

Ashfield flushed very slightly, turned quickly towards the bench. He began playing with a chemical balance and making adjustments to the scale.

Cockfield chuckled.

'But we're all human, Super . . . when the chips are down, eh? You, me, the lot of us. Squeeze the orange and the pips squeak. I've never met a saint – plenty of hypocrites, no saints! Just good triers and bad triers, those are the sizes we come in.

'Me, I never sack a man if there's one damned reason why I shouldn't, and if he's a trier, he's my friend.

'Now what about coming along with me?'

He thrust out a hand, as though expecting Gently to strike it to close the deal. Gently grinned, shrugged feebly. How could one help liking Cockfield?

'All right,' he said. 'I'm sold.'

'That's talking like a man! You've done with Ken?'

'For the moment.'

'Come on. My car is outside.'

'Just one other thing.'

'What's that?'

Cockfield hung on apprehensively.

'That violet muck . . . I think I'll try it. And for chrissake, don't slap my back!'

CHAPTER ELEVEN

THEY WENT OUT to Cockfield's car, a maroon Daimler with slate-coloured upholstery, and Cockfield drove smoothly and patiently along Abbeygate and up the Buttermarket. People spilled off the pavements and darted out from behind parked vehicles. At the Market Place a waving constable was trying to keep the traffic moving.

Cockfield's joviality had waned a little since he'd got into the car, but there was reason enough for that in the difficult *traffic* conditions. Gently felt better. The violet muck – it had tasted like camphorated sulphuric acid – had settled his head, after a preliminary spasm when the top of his skull seemed to have blown off. But now it was apparently back on station, and he had a sensation of floating calm.

They turned down towards the station and then left towards Milehall. Beyond the town the country was park-like and the road fringed with giant trees. Almost, it had a forest atmosphere, with tall plantations in the distance, and the roadside trees, oaks and limes, tangled together high overhead.

'You're not taking me far, are you . . . ?'

'Only to Colton. That's three miles.'

'What's there?'

'You'll see, brother.'

Gently grunted and lit his pipe.

Soon there appeared a right turn beside which was erected a large board. It was painted white with a red border and carried the name: COCKFIELD, in heavy capitals. They turned off. They were on an unfenced road which unravelled its way through a pocket of heath, closed, at a distance, on each side by low thickets or plantations. Bracken and ferns grew on the heath and occasional thorns and flaking pines. One looked continually for outcrops of rock, but there were only burns of sand or gravel.

'Rum country, eh . . . ?'

Gently shrugged, puffed.

'You'll see a cottage in a minute . . . I was born in that cottage.'

They came to it. It was a ruin. It had been built of clay lump. Plaster, slipping off from one side, showed honey-coloured clay in which straw had been mixed. The thatched roof was sagging in, revealing pale edgings of unweathered straw, and a few rotted timbers appeared carcass-like through the gaps. Cockfield drove by without slowing.

'Wasn't any damp-course in those days! Two up, two down, and mother had six children. The old man was a keeper here. He died of rheumatics. We went to

126

school in Abbotsham – three miles. We walked it. All dead except me . . . two died in the war. Tom, he was the last to go. Now I own the whole shoot . . .'

'You mean the cottage . . . ?'

'The whole shoot! Eight hundred acres, thereabouts, and two farms, and the hall. Not that the hall's much to swank about, it was a hospital during the war. The National Trust wouldn't have it. I let it stand there and rot.'

'Couldn't you demolish it for the salvage?'

'I let it rot – while I build!'

Now they swung through a belt of pines and were met suddenly by an open prospect. Straight ahead, on a gentle rise, stood a large Georgian house of yellow brick. At once, even from a distance, one saw the house was falling into dereliction, for a number of the windows lacked frames and the main entrance gaped doorless.

But to the left, a little below them, was a criss-cross area of dug foundations, and beyond these a score of part-finished houses on which men were busily engaged. Farther back still were finished houses grouped in semicircular closes which, at their centres, had each one or two trees, left for effect when the site was cleared.

Children played under the trees and mothers with prams gossiped there. On the building site cement-mixers churned, a tip-lorry discharged a load of sand.

Only the eyeless house on the rise seemed out of place, seemed mistaken.

Cockfield parked. He glanced at Gently.

'Well, Super?'

'Where's this?'

'Colton New Village, that's where. Not a New Town – a New Village.'

'Your idea?'

'Who else's? The County Council wouldn't touch it – not that I wanted them in, anyway! But I put it to them, at the start.'

Cockfield gestured over the wheel.

'I've built this from scratch in eighteen months. Over a hundred houses, a couple of shops, a village hall and made-up roads. Now we're finishing ten houses a week and plan to work up to fifteen. The overall scheme is for five hundred houses with shops, pubs, clinic, a library.

'And when it's finished I'll start again across the other side of the estate.

'There's my answer to the housing problem – houses, brother: houses – houses!'

'Since eighteen months ago you've built this . . . ?'

Cockfield nodded without looking. His big hands gripped the wheel, he stared ahead, massive, heavy.

'What would you say – are they good houses? You bet they are, when I build them! I've dug foundations and carried a hod, I've never skimped a job in my life. Look – look! What would they cost you, twenty miles out of London? Four thousand – five – six – seven?

'I'm charging eighteen-fifty a house!

'Eighteen-fifty, with quarter of an acre, gates, fences, laid path – three bedrooms, two reception, kitchen, garage, part-heating.

'And if you haven't the brass I'll rent you one of my houses. Seven – eight guineas a week? Forty bob, brother, and walk in!'

He lifted his hands and slapped the wheel as though pounding at a rostrum. His body was tense behind the action and he made the whole car quiver.

Gently puffed.

'You're doing it at a loss . . . ?'

'No! That's the cream of the business. I'm making it pay, like a bloody capitalist – enough to put in the public buildings.'

'But it's non-profit-making.'

'Only as far as the money goes. Set that aside and it's pure profit. I'm building houses and gyping nobody.'

'Whose money paid for this Daimler?'

Cockfield relaxed, gave a snorting chuckle.

'I've got a great big house, too, brother – and a weekend place – and a yacht! Ted the Red's a real stinker, eats caviar over his Marx. I'm right and left of the Party line and they hate my guts. I spoil the image.'

'But you do make money.'

'Who says I don't? Sammy Bronstein paid for the car.'

'Who's he?'

'A social criminal – financier, slum-owner, managing director. British Best Buys is his latest floating. They're putting in supermarkets all over the southeast. I'm building them out this way. I can offer what they want – plant, quality, good labour relations and completion on the dot.

'And I soak them for it, brother. I'm a capitalist to a

capitalist. There's just this difference – I never skimp. And they know it. And they pay.'

'So you're a sort of Robin Hood.'

'Do you want me to sing the Red Flag?'

'But you started this village eighteen months ago.'

Cockfield's hands tightened on the wheel.

He looked at Gently, looked away.

'I told you,' he said, 'I rang the station. I got Perkins. He said you were asking about me, about that accident I had. All right. It was a hell of a thing. You don't know how you'll act when it happens. It happened to me. I did the wrong things. I acted like a bastard . . . I was one. It's been on my conscience ever since and I don't think I'll ever stop paying for it. Once it's done there's no undoing it. You just have to live with what you are.'

Gently didn't say anything. Cockfield drew a heavy breath. Now the hands were lying dead towards the bottom of the wheel.

Outside, two youngsters were chasing each other through the bracken at the roadside; they sighted the Daimler and came to a stand, gazing at the car with round eyes.

'I didn't know the kid. I knew his father, he's in the post office. But I knew the kid's girl friend, Jenny Morris, she's the daughter of one of my foremen.

'We have a social club, I sometimes go there . . . you know, I like to be close to the men . . . I knew Jenny. She was a lovely kid. It knocked her flat. She's gone teaching in Canada.

130

'People see it from the outside – what they read in the papers.

'That way, it's easy to condemn . . . or you, hearing just an outline . . .'

'So this village . . . ?'

Cockfield shook his head vigorously.

'What connection can there be? They're two separate things, they don't cancel out – nothing ever cancels out.

'Though if I dared, I tell you this, I'd call it the Clifford Amies Village . . . but what the devil good would it do? What good would it do Jenny Morris?

'No! You just can't cancel things out. You can accept them, that's about all. If you can learn a bit . . . not to condemn . . . that's about it. That's the size.'

'Yet someone condemned Peter Shimpling.'

'He—'

Cockfield bit his lip.

'He was a rat, you were going to say, a predatory animal. He didn't deserve to have his life.'

'I wasn't going to say that! My God, that's the sort of thing I fight against. You don't understand. I didn't condemn him. But now it's done, can't be undone.'

'So we should forget it?'

'I know you can't. But how are you ever going to understand it? You see, the essence of it . . . the basic facts . . . you're barking up the wrong tree. Yes, somebody did condemn Shimpling, somebody loosed the tiger on him. Those are facts, but you're letting them blind you – say you've stumbled on them from the wrong angle.'

'What's the right angle?'

'How should I know?'

'You're pretty certain I've got the wrong one.'

'I am. I live here, I know the people, know the feel of it. You don't know that.'

'Is that all you know?'

'I'm trying to help you! If only I could put you on the right track . . . However much you know, you're bound to be wrong, and you might make a mess for which you'd be sorry. Why do you think I grabbed you this morning?'

'Frankly . . . ?'

'Yes.'

'You'd like to square me.'

'Call it that – I'm not squeamish! Perhaps you think I've done it before?'

Gently shrugged. 'It wouldn't have been necessary, not if I heard the story right. But you may have got hold of the impression, locally, that the police'll swallow a good cover-up.'

Cockfield was dragging on the wheel again. Now he thumped it with his palms.

'All right – I deserve that, very probably. I don't care – throw it at me! But it's not the reason, the whole reason. I brought you out here to give you a hint. Oh, I know how you're working things out, making two and two equal four – and you're right, you're getting at the facts – but you're wrong too. That's my point!

'No, listen. You're full of sharp questions – was there ever a policeman who wasn't? – you sort out a case like a box of tricks while the locals here just fumble. But are they wrong and you right? Isn't it better to fumble sometimes? To let a weed wither away instead of trampling on the corn? Especially – this is worth considering – if you have any doubt about the weed?

'You've seen Abbotsham. You think it's slow. We don't know what makes London tick. But do you know what makes us tick – the sort of people we are here? Because that's important, more important than the facts you're following up – a perspective, you understand – an elevation, as well as the plans.

'Have you checked the crime figures for Abbotsham? No? You didn't think to do that?

'A manslaughter, a burglary and a bigamy – they were the highspots of 62.

'And that's Abbotsham. A good place to live, where people have time to like each other – a place where nothing ever happens because we're too damn busy living our lives! Plenty of money, no slums, a little culture, a lot of decency. And small enough – we know each other, aren't just ants in a heap.

'Whoever heard of blackmailing in Abbotsham before this fast boy came down from London?'

Gently shifted a little. 'What are you trying to say?'

'Nothing! Just giving you the perspective – no more than that. Shimpling comes here, ferrets about, finds he's on virgin soil, begins to put the bite on people, to spread his poison through Abbotsham. And some devil loses his head and that's the lot for Shimpling – wrong, perhaps, but it happened – and the pity was it didn't end there.

'The question is, how wrong?'

133

Gently shook his head. 'Not a question for me.'

Cockfield turned, looked at him. 'But it is,' he said. 'Believe me, the whole business turns on that. Suppose it wasn't murder?'

Gently said nothing.

'Suppose it was . . .' Cockfield hesitated. 'If it were . . . in some way . . . less than murder, would it be worthwhile blowing the lid off?'

'Less than murder in what way?'

Cockfield patted the wheel. 'I don't know! More like . . . manslaughter, something of that sort.'

'Can you suggest how it could have been man-slaughter?'

Cockfield twisted. 'Well . . . it might have been an accident. Perhaps they only meant to scare the fellow.'

'They?'

'Him, her, who you like! It's as reasonable an assumption as another.'

Gently shook his head again. 'I wouldn't hang my hopes on that. The way it was done wasn't to throw a scare, and throwing a scare wouldn't have solved any problems. If Shimpling had survived he'd have had another sting, would maybe have taken his revenge. The tiger was put in there to kill him. Nothing else will stand up.'

'But if there was any question . . . ?'

'I can't make bargains.'

'But you can suppose—'

'I'd rather stick to the facts! How much had you drunk on the night you killed Amies?'

Cockfield clung to the wheel, said nothing.

Gently said: 'You were being blackmailed. Ashfield and Hastings were being blackmailed. You claim to have spent that night together and your alibis cancel out. Groton was also being blackmailed and so was Sayers and a certain lady. Put it into any perspective you like, and what's a policeman going to think?'

'I don't know about the others—'

'Don't give me the parrot cry again! We're combing the country for Shimpling's girlfriend, and she'll talk, and that'll be that.'

'As a witness in court—'

'How did Shimpling get on to you?'

'I never set eyes on the damn fellow!'

'I think he was clever enough to bluff you. He probably had nothing on you at all.'

'I tell you I never met him!'

'This is the way I'd say it happened. Straight after you were charged at the magistrates' court you received a letter marked "Private and Confidential". It said the writer had information about where you'd been before the accident, and that if you didn't want him to go to the police you'd pass him a small sum in notes. What did you do – pay up?'

'I didn't—'

'You hadn't much option, had you? A squeak of that sort would have finished you – Mayor, bigwig, public benefactor! And the fellow wasn't asking so much, or so you thought at the time – oh yes, you slipped him the money quick. You were even glad that he was crooked.

'Then after the case, what happened? Another one

135

of those damned letters! But this time you thought it safe to defy him and you didn't pass the money. So, he cracked the whip with an anonymous letter that sent Amies's father on the rampage, and before you knew how it happened you were coughing up a regular monthly payment.

'And my guess is it was pure bluff. He didn't know anything – except human nature.'

'Listen, Superintendent—'

'Isn't that how it was?'

Cockfield's knuckles were pale on the wheel.

'I don't say it was, don't say it wasn't – but I still say you might make a fool of yourself!'

'That's a risk I'll take. Now tell me – where's Sayers?'

'Sayers . . . ?'

'Yes – and don't say Bournemouth! My bet is he's not far away – could be here, in one of your houses.'

'No – not here.'

'But you know where he is?'

Suddenly not only Cockfield's knuckles were pale.

'Sayers . . . he retired.'

'Oh yes, I dare say. And oddly enough, soon after the murder.'

'I – I don't know.'

He'd gone quite still, staring ahead at the crescents of houses. As with Hastings yesterday, the mention of Sayers seemed to touch a button . . . and wasn't this one fear? Sweat was misting on his slanted forehead.

'You'd have known him, of course?'

'Oh yes, I knew him. In my line of business . . . well, we had several deals.'

'In fact, you'd known him for a number of years?'

'Well yes . . . we both belong here.'

'Yet you've not a notion where he's retired to – he didn't as much as send you a card?'

Cockfield squirmed. 'Dave had letters from him – Dave Hastings who bought him out! Dave says he went to Bournemouth. I don't know any more than that. *I* wasn't bosom friends with the man, he didn't have to tell me anything. If you want him, why not look for him?'

Gently nodded. 'We're doing just that.'

The tip-lorry backed out of the site and came up the road towards them. The beefy, blond-haired man who drove it leaned out grinning and made a V-sign. Cockfield lifted a big hand in acknowledgement. The lorry went on towards Abbotsham. A smell of sand, of mortar, drifted momentarily in through the Daimler's window.

'They'll have those houses finished,' Cockfield said, then, without a change of tone: 'You're a bloody devil!'

Gently shrugged. 'I'm a trier,' he said. 'And I don't like any sort of murderer.'

'And you'll go by the book,' Cockfield said.

Gently nodded. 'By the book. Though it blasts your crime-free town wide open, I'll have the man who killed Shimpling.'

'Even . . . though it does more harm than good?'

Gently looked at him. Cockfield avoided the look.

CHAPTER TWELVE

C OCKFIELD DROPPED GENTLY outside Headquarters
without having said very much on the return
journey. His rather fish-like face had a droop in it, as
though that hangover had at last caught up with him.
Finally he said, as Gently slammed the door:

'Will you be around if someone wants to get in
touch with you . . . ?'

But somehow it didn't come out like a question, and
when Gently didn't answer Cockfield drove off
immediately.

Obviously, he was going hot-foot to consult someone — which would perhaps take him into Dutt's
sphere of observation! Gently smiled to himself: he
hadn't been wasting his time. He had a comfortable
feeling that things were on the move . . .

Two of the reporters' cars were parked opposite
Headquarters and when Gently went in a head popped
out of the waiting-room.

'Anything for the evenings, chiefie?'

Gently strolled over and looked through the door.

Three other pressmen sat round a table, each holding a hand of cards. Cigarettes hung angled from their mouths and the air in the room was a haze of smoke. On the table was a kitty of cash which they hadn't bothered to hide.

'You're a cheeky lot of so-and-so's, aren't you?'

'Aw, chiefie – it's a dog's life!'

'At least you could have a paper ready to plonk down on that lolly.'

One of the card-players reached wearily behind him to where his jacket hung over a chair, took out a paper, unfolded it, spread it over the pile of money.

'OK, chiefie?'

'Make it show the sports page.'

'That's hamming it, chiefie!'

'Anyway, what are you blokes doing here – why aren't you setting the cops an example?'

A thin-faced man sucked in air but blew smoke through his nostrils.

'We're overhanded,' he said. 'There's half the Street sculling around here. Some of the boys are out digging. Some are out dating blondes. Some are playing peep-bo with Groton. We're just here waiting for handouts. What have you got, chiefie?'

'Yes – what have you got?'

'I've a good mind to walk off with the kitty.'

'Don't be like that, chiefie!'

Gently sighed. 'Couldn't you open just one of those windows?'

He sucked a moment on his dead pipe, then said:

'So you're still watching Groton.'

The thin-faced man narrowed his eyes.

'We're manning the fox-holes,' he said.

'Any more shooting?'

'Just routine. He likes to fire off a gun. One of the boys picked a shot out of his trousers, but that'd be a richochet. We're not scoring it.'

'Anyone know where he went last night?'

'We were hoping you could tell us. He bashed a headlamp, knocked some glass out. But maybe he didn't get to reporting it.'

'Who saw that?'

'One of the bimbos who was prowling round early this morning. Charlie Slater. Takes pics for the *Sun*. Then Groton started blasting, Slater started running. Would it be something?'

'Not unless Charlie Slater got perforated. Did he get a photograph?'

'Uhuh. We get anything on Groton?'

Gently looked at the thin-faced man curiously.

'Why are you so set on Groton?' he asked.

The man nostrilled smoke.

'Instinct,' he said. 'Come rain, come snow, we know he did it. Have you busted his alibi?'

Gently shook his head.

'One of these days you'll have to bust it.'

'It won't bust.'

'It has to bust. This job has Groton written all over it.'

Gently hunched a shoulder. 'I'll give you that, but don't let it raise any hopes. Unless the entire Safari Club is underwriting him, Groton was in London when Shimpling bought it. You know the Safari Club?'

'What do you think?'

'Groton was attending their committee meeting on that night. With two peers, a cabinet minister and the MP for Kemptown West.'

'We still like Groton.'

'Facts are facts – those things that editors scream for.'

'So why not give us some facts?'

Gently hunched again. 'All right. We're looking for a man called Samuel Sayers . . .'

He grinned at the thin-faced man, who said automatically:

'You got any pics?'

'A pic. I'll swap it with you – for Slater's pic of the bashed headlamp.'

But when Gently entered Perkins's office he found the local man at his most lugubrious and was greeted with:

'Sayers has skipped! He's cleared his account and gone abroad.'

Gently sighed, sat himself, made a business of filling his pipe. How had Perkins ever got into that habit of expressing vast dismay with his chubby features? Relaxed, they were naturally cheerful, had a rounded, child-like optimism. But at the first sign of a check . . .

Was that what Abbotsham did to a man?

He blew smoke at the ceiling.

'Sure he's gone abroad?' he asked.

'What else can one think? Bournemouth is check-ing, but . . . Do you think we should inform Interpol?'

'Not just yet! What have we got?'

'Hargrave traced his account to the National and District.'

Hargrave, a square-shouldered, ruddy-faced man, sat glumly to the right of Perkins's desk.

He said: 'Sayers had deposit and current accounts, sir. He had over twenty thou in the deposit account. On twentieth September last year he wrote from Bournemouth asking to have his account transferred there.'

'From what address?'

'From a hotel, sir, The Stansgate in Marine Parade. He said he proposed to settle in Bournemouth and was looking over some properties.'

'Have Bournemouth checked?'

'Yes sir. But he was only at The Stansgate for a weekend. He came back afterwards to ask for letters, but didn't leave any address.'

'Go on.'

'Well, the bank rang their Bournemouth branch, sir, and the address they had was in Boscombe. But that was a furnished holiday bungalow which he only took for a month. By that time he'd emptied his accounts by cheques in favour of the Unit Finance Company. It was at one-month call, sir, and he drew it in cash in November. The UFC had an address at Southbourne. It was another furnished property.'

'Well?'

Hargrave shrugged. 'I'm afraid that's it, sir. He left no address with the letting agent.'

'He's skipped abroad!' Perkins moaned. 'It's obvious, that's what it was building up to.'

'He was covering his tracks,' Gently said.

'He didn't have any connections over here. He'd have changed his name, bought a forged passport . . . probably he's in the south of France.'

'But he *was* at Bournemouth . . .'

'In November!'

Gently puffed once or twice. He could have sworn that Hastings had lied to them about Sayers . . . in fact, what interest had he in telling them the truth?

If Sayers was the 'third man' in the business, the one who'd actually done the job, surely Hastings should have done his best . . . Yet at once he'd mentioned Bournemouth!

'Let's go over this again. A month after the tiger business Sayers is in Bournemouth. He appears only just to have arrived there and he stays at a hotel while he makes his arrangements. At once he writes to his bank – without waiting till he has a more permanent address – so that he has to return to the hotel to collect the bank's reply.

'Why do that? Presumably on the next day he finds and moves into the holiday bungalow – a project presenting no difficulty at that end of the season. So why not defer his letter till then? What was the hurry about?'

'If he were short of money . . .'

'How could that be? He wouldn't have left Abbotsham empty-handed.'

'He might have gone somewhere else first . . . perhaps he skipped straight away, in Shimpling's car.'

'Still, he'd have his cheque book with him, and his pals here would have slipped him money. And if he was scared of going back to Abbotsham, he should have been just as scared of writing to his bank.

'But what was he scared of, anyway – when the killing hadn't come to light?'

Perkins shook his head woefully. 'It's a bit of a mystery, that is . . .'

Gently blew a stream of smoke. 'All right, then a bit of a mystery. It may mean something, may mean nothing. Next, having got his account at Bournemouth, he empties it by cheques made out to a trust company – which he could have done just as easily while the account was still at Abbotsham. Again, why?'

'Perhaps . . .'

'Of course – plenty of adventitious reasons! He may not have thought of the trust company dodge until he'd had the account transferred. Or again, the local bank manager would know him, might want to discuss the investment, while to the Bournemouth man he was simply a name and there wouldn't be that bother. Plenty of reasons. All I'm emphasizing is that we have a need to suppose one.

'After that it's straightforward, if Sayers's motive was to vanish. He's shifted his capital into an investment which he can cash without questions asked. Once it's cashed he's broken the link; we can no longer trace him through his money. He reinvests it in another name, in another place, from another address.

'Man and money are both gone . . .'

'Would it matter if we traced him to Bournemouth?'

Perkins heaved a sigh from deep down. 'He's our chummie all right,' he said. 'He wouldn't have done all this . . . yet he wasn't a bad sort of fellow. We'll have to get him, fetch him back. He'll be abroad, I'm certain. He took a Lads' Club party to France one year . . . he'll know all the ropes.'

'Did he have a car?' Gently asked Hargrave.

'Sorry, sir . . . I haven't checked yet.'

Gently reached for the phone, asked the board for Hastings's office. It was the girl who answered.

'I'm afraid Mr Hastings is out . . .'

'Never mind, miss. Perhaps you can tell me – what sort of car had Sam Sayers?'

A black Hillman, she told him. Not new, not old. He'd kept it in the garage at the rear of the office. Yes, of course he'd taken it with him when he vacated the flat. How did she know? Because Mr Hastings had moved there and had begun using the garage.

Gently pushed the phone to Hargrave.

'Get the registration number from the Licence Office, then put out a general call. It may lead us to something. When you've done that try the tax people and the National Insurance Office.

'Probably they won't know anything – but that'll tell us something, too.'

Hargrave took the phone, began dialling.

'Really, he was quite a decent sort . . .' Perkins groaned.

'Some murderers are,' Gently snapped. 'Anyway, Sayers wasn't an angel.'

'Just one slip . . .'

Gently hammered out his pipe, filled it again and relit it. Perkins winced and shut up. At least, he was beginning to know his Gently . . .

145

But suddenly he flushed crimson and started to forage among the papers on the desk.

'My God . . . I forgot! Just before Hargrave got back . . . this came for you over the phone . . .'

'Thanks very much.'

'It went out of my head . . . all I could think about was Sayers!'

He handed the report to Gently with a pink hand that actually trembled.

It came from Ferrow. He was no farther forward in his attempts to trace Cheyne-Chevington. He recommended sending down Cheyne-Chevington's ex-housekeeper to make the necessary identification. Nor had they pulled in Shirley Banks, but they were on a hot scent. She'd been seen in Fulham as recently as yesterday and Division was making exhaustive inquiries.

'Did you read this?' Gently asked.

'Yes . . . it wasn't urgent, was it?'

'Where's that report about Shimpling's car?'

'I had it here . . . there it is!'

'Where was it sold?'

'Peckthorne's Garage—'

'I know about that! Fulham, wasn't it?'

'Yes, Fulham.'

'And now we find Shimpling's girlfriend turning up there.'

Gently puffed at his pipe fiercely.

'Look – during all your preliminary fact-gathering – did you turn up any information to show when Banks actually left Shimpling?'

'We talked to the tradesmen . . .'

'What did they tell you?'

'They hadn't seen her for several weeks. Usually, she took the goods in, paid the bills. Then, afterwards, Shimpling did it.'

'From which they deduced she wasn't there?'

'Well . . . that seemed reasonable.'

'But it could simply mean she wasn't there, say, on Saturdays, when the goods were delivered, the bills paid?'

Perkins was going red again.

'Yes . . . I suppose . . . we're not certain . . .'

'And she might have been there all the time – and at last, taken off in Shimpling's car?'

Perkins gaped at him. 'Yes . . . of course! There isn't any reason why not . . . just . . .'

'Which shortly afterwards was sold in Fulham – where Shirley Banks was seen yesterday.'

'But how . . . why?'

Gently shook his head. 'That's what we'll find out when we catch up with her. Suddenly, I'd sooner have a talk with Shirley than I would even with Sam Sayers.

'She's the key-piece. She may have been an eye-witness to what happened at the bungalow. She may have had a finger in it, too – that's not beyond credibility.'

'Not in the murder!'

'Why not? Who could have helped them plot it better?'

'But not a woman . . . in that business!'

Gently gazed at him, puffing.

147

'As I see it, there are several possibilities to keep in mind, and it's no use your murmuring "Sayers is a decent fellow" to yourself. The odds are heavy that he was chummie, the one who actually let loose the tiger – and if he was capable of that, what else might he not have done?

'For instance, we think we're dealing with a dead blackmailer. We could be dealing with a live one! We've no proof that Shimpling's killer destroyed the material he found in the bungalow. Sayers may have vanished for another reason – to avoid the fate that caught up with Shimpling. While, from an accommodation address, the demands continue as before . . .

'But that's only one possibility. Shirley Banks represents another. She, too, may have had an opportunity to grab the blackmail material.

'And in her case, consider this: she was living out there with a queer. Isn't it likely she'd establish . . . more satisfactory relations, with someone else?

'With, for example, a huge hunk of male, like the womanizing Hugh Groton . . . ?

'No – you'll be a fool if you rule her out because she's a woman.'

'But she . . . Groton . . . !' Perkins stammered.

'Just bear it in mind, that's my advice. Don't lock people up in watertight compartments and kid yourself they're going to stay there. That way you'll only puzzle yourself and make a mystery of the plainest evidence. People are icebergs. Below the surface there's eight-ninths you never see.'

Perkins was stuck. He goggled at Gently, his mouth

open as though to catch something. Poor fellow! Perhaps never again would he have his ideas jolted like this. His world of blacks and whites was adequate for the routine days of Abbotsham . . . this was the great case of his career. How much of it could he understand?

Hargrave laid down the phone, but almost immediately it began ringing. He listened a moment, then said to Gently:

'Somebody asking for you, sir?'

Gently took it.

'Who's speaking . . . ?'

'It's me – Hastings. You know my voice.'

'What do you want?'

Hastings hesitated. 'I want to talk to you . . . not on the phone.'

'Where are you speaking from?'

'Weston-le-Willows. I want you to meet me out here.'

'What's wrong with your office?'

'Every damned thing! Doesn't that man of yours ever report?'

'I see,' Gently said. 'And the lady wants to speak to me too.'

'Yes. But don't bring that bloody fool Perkins, or you won't get a word from either of us.'

Gently turned to hide his face from Perkins.

'I'll bring my inspector. That all right?'

'If you must. But nobody else.'

'At Cockfield's chalet?'

'Yes.'

'I'll be there.'

He hung up.

Hargrave was studying a clip of orders that hung on the wall. Perkins, beetroot again, was chewing his thumbnail.

Poor Perkins! He'd heard.

CHAPTER THIRTEEN

I T WAS NOON when Gently tooled through the traffic in his Rover 105. As he passed the Jew's House the clock was tolling and the sound came to him faintly. Also he smelled, skirting the market, a tantalizing whiff of fried onion, suggesting that the stall with a smoking chimney was busy dispensing hot dogs.

A pity, in a way, he was here on business! Very reluctantly, he was liking Abbotsham – getting the feel of the place, you'd say, getting with it, the different tempo.

Now, as he parked in the Buttermarket, he sat for a moment before getting out to fetch Dutt, watching dreamily while people pushed past with their big baskets and queer-shaped parcels.

And wasn't there football this afternoon – Southern League, something of that sort?

Because of a breeze setting from the Market Place he could still smell those fried onions . . .

In the end he didn't have to fetch Dutt because Dutt had seen the Rover and come down. He appeared at the window looking hot and bored — doubtless, he'd had his fill of the Buttermarket!

'Anything new, chief?'

'Hop in, Dutt.'

Dutt walked round and got in.

'It's been pretty quiet, chief,' he said. 'Nothing but customers all the morning.'

'Did Cockfield come here?' Gently asked.

'What does he look like, chief?'

'Age late fifties, big build, wearing an Irish tweed two-piece and a squash hat.'

'Drives a maroon Daimler?'

'That's him.'

'Yes, he was here about five to eleven.'

'Tell me what you saw.'

'He went straight up to Hastings's office. I thought he was a customer having a row.'

'How was that?'

'Well . . . he didn't sit down, just stood there laying down the law. Then Hastings jumped up and they seemed to have an argument. But it was all over in five minutes.'

'Then did Hastings use the phone?'

'Yes, as soon as the other man went. Then Hastings came down and said something to the girl, then he went through to the back. That's the last I've seen of him.'

Gently chuckled. 'Now you're going to see some more of him — not to mention that *Debrett* blonde of yours.'

'You mean Lady Laura?'

'Herself in person.'

Dutt whistled. 'I knew I should have changed my tie.'

While they drove out to Weston-le-Willows Gently filled Dutt in on the morning's events. Weston was ten miles out of Abbotsham and remote from the principal roads.

Departing from the wold-like sweeps about the town one entered a miniature, toy-like countryside, with little humpy fields, tall hawthorn hedges and top-heavy cottages with steep straw thatch.

Yes, a picture-book country! You almost found yourself saying: 'This is a cow, a barn, a bow-wow.' Even the colours seemed specially simple, brilliant-lit and glowing.

At one point they descended to a ford, flowing through a cauldron-like den of trees. A cloud of white butterflies, settled there drinking, scoldingly rose as the car washed by them.

Again, poised perfectly on a hill, as though placed there deliberately for an artist to paint, a post-mill pressed its sails to the sky and the rounded clouds with their purplish-brown bases.

From here, these cottages, these farmhouses, came the big baskets to the Saturday market . . .

Then they passed out of this fairy-tale country into a flatter, more fenny area, where the cottages, coloured yellow, white or blue, were partly hidden among groves of willow.

A signpost said: 'Weston ½'.

Gently pulled up alongside a parked tractor.

153

'I'm looking for Ted Cockfield's place . . .'

'Go straight through the village, then bear to your right.'

Gently drove through the village. Here, besides cottages, were houses of timber, plaster and pantiles. The single shop had a sagging bow window stuffed with saucepans, knitting wools and canned goods.

Near the church a lane forked to the right and was posted simply: 'Fen Street'. It passed through a screen of very tall willows beyond which water glimmered through dense reed thickets. Then came three contemporary bungalows, set back in the trees, where the land was higher; and finally, ahead, a big chalet-bungalow, with a circular drive in which were parked two cars.

'Hastings's Jag – and a blue Mercedes!'

They stood bonnet to bonnet, as though conversing.

'Come in.'

Hastings must have been watching for them, since he'd opened the door before Gently had parked. Now, exceedingly dapper in a dark grey lounge suit, he stood aside politely to let them enter.

'You're quite alone?'

'There's just us.'

'It's reporters I'm really worried about.'

Gently shrugged. 'We weren't followed. I'd given them a hand-out before you rang.'

'In that case . . .'

He closed the door and led them down a wide hall. At the bottom were double doors of panelled oak with bottle-glass rounds set in the panels. He opened these and they passed through. The room beyond was a large sun lounge. It had a sweep of plate glass opposite the doors and looked down a lawn to a staithe and a boathouse. At the staithe was moored an awninged yacht and behind it, across the river, towered some huge poplars.

'Let me introduce you. Lady Buxhall.'

Precisely what had Gently expected? If he'd written it down before he came in it would probably have read: 'A born divorcée.'

But she wasn't that type. She didn't have eyes that smiled along with lips that didn't: she lacked the aura of mental eroticism, of physical unreticence.

She was a tall woman, slender and leggy, with appealingly sincere green eyes. Her honey-coloured hair was cut simply and she wore a tailored costume of hyacinth blue.

And she was shy! Although her model training showed in the automatic grace of her movements.

When she shook hands, she did it hurriedly and with a nervous smile that faded quickly.

'Please sit down. David wants to talk to you. We don't have much time.'

She pointed to a semicircle of padded tub chairs which were grouped round a coffee table.

'Drinks?'

'Not for us.'

'You don't mind if we do?'

She went hastily to a cabinet at the end of the room. Hastings, meanwhile, had remained standing near the doors, suddenly tight-mouthed and still.

Gently sat himself in one of the tub chairs and Dutt took another. A pane was tilted in the glass wall but the room was still far too warm. It smelled of stale cigar smoke, of whisky. A folded card table stood by the drinks cabinet.

Lady Buxhall returned with glasses.

'Dave?'

'No . . . I'm not drinking.'

She stood holding the glases indecisively for a moment, then set them down on the coffee table.

Hastings came forward.

'I've asked you here—' he began. Then he looked at Lady Buxhall. 'Oh hell!' he said. 'This'll tell you quickest!' And he caught her to him in a fierce embrace.

He kissed her, slowly, intensely.

'There . . .' he said. 'Am I making it plain? You believe your own eyes, do you – there's no lies about this?'

'Dave, darling . . .' Lady Buxhall protested, pushing him away from her.

'I'm sorry, Lolly – but this was necessary. You don't know these people like I do.'

He turned to Gently.

'Well,' he said. 'Have I proved anything to you?'

Gently sketched the ghost of a shrug. 'Yes . . . I'm beginning to think you have.'

'I love Laura. I've always loved her. This isn't some nasty little intrigue. I want to marry her like hell – and, by heaven, I *am* going to marry her. I'd have married her years ago, only she had the good sense to quit on me.'

Gently glanced at Laura Buxhall.

'Yes,' she said quietly. 'That's true. David asked me to marry him then. Such a long time ago.'

'Before she ever met Buxhall – that's what I want you to understand. Because I know what you must have been thinking – the Buxhall millions and all that. But you're wrong. It's nothing of that sort. I'm not in this for any money. I want Laura and nothing else just Laura. Just Laura!'

'All right,' Gently said. 'Calm down.'

'I want you to tell me you believe that.'

'If you'll tell me—'

'No – no conditions.'

Gently spread his hands. 'All right – I believe it.'

David Hastings patted his brow, and now he did reach for the drink. He picked it up with an unsteady hand. But he only sipped a drop from it.

'Suppose you sit down,' Gently said.

'I'd rather stand, if you don't mind. What I'd sooner do is smash something.'

'That won't help things very much.'

'I'm not so sure.'

He sipped another drop. He compressed his lips and looked at Gently.

'I can guess what you started to ask me,' he said. 'And there's a one-word answer to it. Yes.'

'You are Dr Cheyne-Chevington?'

'Yes. Or I was, four years ago.'

'Can you prove identity?'

'Here's my passport.'

He took it from his pocket and handed it to Gently.

In the passport photograph Hastings had no beard and his moustache was more luxuriant, but the features were little changed and the expression of the eyes was unmistakable.

'Why are you telling me this now?'

'I should have thought it's pretty obvious.'

'Not to me.'

'Oh my God! Laura's about to file her divorce.'

Lady Buxhall said: 'There's another woman involved. My husband has been seeing her over a period of months. I hoped, when I had evidence, he would give her up, but he refuses. And I love David.'

'Well?'

'My husband doesn't want to let me go.'

'He's proud of Laura,' Hastings exclaimed. 'This other woman is around fifty – having Laura boosts his beastly ego.'

Gently nodded. 'So he'll defend.'

'Of course. If he has anything to go on. And if he sends detectives poking around he'll find enough evidence for a shrewd lawyer.'

'And so you want to make a deal.'

'Isn't that what I'm trying to say?'

'On Cockfield's advice . . .'

'To hell with Cockfield! I'm offering you facts – isn't that enough?'

Gently rocked his shoulders. 'Ah well, I should be getting used to Abbotsham methods. If Shimpling had picked them up sooner he might have done a deal with the tiger.'

'Just keep Laura out of it – that's all we ask.'

'And in return, you'll come clean?'

'As far as I can.'

'Which won't be very far.'

'As far as I can. I can't offer more.'

'Right,' Gently said. 'Now for heaven's sake, sit. There's been enough Scotch spilt on this carpet. I'm offering you nothing. It's up to you. But I didn't come down here to upset any divorces.'

'Fair enough,' Hastings said.

He took one of the tub chairs facing Gently.

'I was Dr Cheyne-Chevington,' he said, 'and I knew Shimpling, and he was blackmailing me. That's the reason why I changed my identity and came up here in the first place. You'll know about the trial. That charge was based on false evidence. Shimpling fabricated it because I played tough and resisted his demands. Whether the charge stuck or not didn't matter, it was ruin for me as a professional man, and I daren't come out in the open about the blackmail because it affected Laura here.

'I'll have to tell you about that. Laura came to me as a patient in 56. After that I saw a lot of her and did my best to persuade her to marry me. She refused – and she was right. To be frank, I was a pretty wild lot in those days – I was mixed up with a peculiar set, and I dare say the crash was coming in any case. I took Laura about to some of those parties and the poor girl was shocked by what went on – and well, she quit, and soon after that Buxhall began to lay siege to her.

'All right – I deserved it: it knocked some sense into

159

my head. And if I wanted any further sobering-up, there was Shimpling waiting on my doorstep. He'd also been to one of the parties and he'd managed to take a photograph, and he threatened to sell it to a scandal sheet unless I paid him a thousand pounds.

'What he didn't know – thank God! – was that Laura was also on the photograph. If it had been published, and Buxhall's family had seen it, they'd have crucified Laura. But I knew, and I knew I'd have to get that photograph somehow. I felt pretty certain I wouldn't get it merely by paying Shimpling his demand.'

Hastings broke off, stared hard at Gently.

'Suppose I admitted to pinching it?' he said.

Gently pulled a face. 'We'd want proof,' he said. 'I doubt whether we'd get it, after so long.'

Hastings nodded. 'Right. I pinched it. Shimpling made a mistake in coming to me personally. I knocked him out and took his keys and searched his car and found the negative. And I'd have burgled his flat too, if I hadn't found it in the car. But that's where it was, locked in the boot, along with a couple more prints.

'So I destroyed them before his eyes – while he was swearing bloody murder. And he meant it. Twenty-four hours later a CID man came to check my drug-book.'

He darted a look at Laura Buxhall, but she sat gazing at the glass she held. Her colour was high . . . but of course it was warm, there in the south-facing sun lounge.

Gently said: 'You were given Not Guilty. How was it you came to be struck off?'

Hastings laughed shortly. 'You should read up the evidence. Merely being innocent wasn't going to help me. Shimpling had plenty of hard stuff about parties and orgies and classy prostitutes. Oh, my neck was stuck out, anyway. Perhaps I wasn't cut out to be a physician.'

'But at least, after the trial, you'd be clear of Shimpling.'

'That's just the devil of it – I wasn't! In the meantime Shimpling had been doing some homework and he'd discovered about Laura. Now he was threatening to inform the Buxhalls that Laura was mixed up in my scandal – threatening me, of course. I had money. Laura wasn't vulnerable till she married.

'What could I do? This time it wasn't a question of knocking him down and grabbing the evidence. He was the evidence – he was notorious for knowing the details of my misconduct. So I paid him. He promised it was to be his one and only demand. I knew it wouldn't be, and I did the only thing possible – I vanished.'

'Yes,' Gently said. 'You did a good job.'

Hastings shrugged. 'It had to be good. If you're thinking I may have cut some corners, well, I may have. That's up to you.'

'Not my department,' Gently said. 'I'd rather hear how you came to Abbotsham.'

Hastings laughed again. 'Chance,' he said. 'Whenever I gamble, I lose.

'My father was an estate agent at Bude, so I knew a little about the business. I decided I'd go in for that and

I looked for something in the professional paper. I found an agency being offered at Abbotsham. It was miles away from my connections. I rang Sayers and got details and settled the matter the same day. I simply went. A very good friend of mine wound up my affairs in Kensington. How was I to know I was going to the one place where Shimpling was bound to find me again?'

He sipped his drink, almost indignantly.

'The swine had another victim at Abbotsham,' he said. 'For six months, I really thought I'd slipped him. Then one day I met him in the street.'

'How did you know Groton was another victim?'

Hastings went still. 'Oh no,' he said. 'It was worth a try, but it's not coming off. I didn't mention any names.'

'We know about Groton.'

'Good for you. But I'm not giving any names.'

'It was Groton you meant.'

'No names.'

Gently sighed. 'Carry on!'

Hastings sipped some more. 'Shimpling sounded me out. He didn't know if he could still swing Laura on me. I tried hard to bluff him but he was too sharp and threatened to try his luck with Laura. Then of course I had to give in. By that time Laura was Lady Buxhall. I hadn't seen her since the trial . . . ironically, it was Shimpling who brought us together again!

'What he wanted now was not, at first, money, but a place at Abbotsham where he could live. He told me that business was improving in Abbotsham and that he

162

intended to move there to watch his investments. He wanted a quiet place — nothing expensive! — somewhere handy but unobtrusive. I had Young's bungalow on the books. I showed him that. He took it.'

'So you're actually the owner of that bungalow?'

Hastings nodded. 'I bought it. Young is living near Derby now. Owles and Porteous did the conveyancing.'

'But surely . . . haven't you been back there?'

Hastings closed his eyes, said: 'Never.'

'Why not?'

'Why should I? Do you think it's a place of happy memory?'

Gently said: 'Put it like this. Suddenly Shimpling disappears. You own the bungalow — wouldn't you repossess it, perhaps sell it to get your money back?'

'I might have done. But I didn't.'

'So why not?'

Hastings shrugged. 'To start with, nobody would have bought it from me. It had been on the books for twelve years.'

'So you left it to rot.'

'That's about it.'

'Wouldn't it have been safer to set light to it?'

'Perhaps. I wouldn't know, would I?'

'You would if you'd looked inside the door.'

Hastings twirled his glass, saying nothing. His handsome face had no expression. He sat easily, almost relaxedly, one well-trained leg crossing the other. At last he said:

'This means nothing, I'm just throwing away some

lines. Different things happen to different people, different people have different reactions. If something happens to you, you understand it. Somebody it hasn't happened to, doesn't. All you can do then is to point out to him that different things happen to different people.'

'And you risked not going back to the bungalow?'

'As I said, I was throwing away lines.'

'Don't throw them away too often,' Gently said. 'You might find twelve other people waiting to catch them.'

Hastings inclined his head. 'Now may I go on?'

'Yes – but it's a question we may come back to.'

Laura Buxhall said: 'I think it's my turn. I've something to tell you about Shimpling.'

She was leaning forward, not looking at Gently, her legs tucked back and to one side. A very faint scent of lily of the valley must have had its origin with her. She spoke haltingly.

'I don't know how much people have told you about Shimpling – people who knew him, I mean – what he was like, the man himself. Well, he was – evil: that's the only word. It was almost as though you could smell it. Not that you could smell it, of course . . . he used cosmetics, just like a tart.

'Yet he wasn't effeminate to look at – from a distance, he appeared quite manly – all the same, there was something wrong, something indecent . . . you seemed to smell it! As though under the flesh he was rotten, neither a man nor a woman. He made you shiver, you couldn't help it. He had eyes like a ferret's. They glittered.'

'When did you meet him?' Gently asked.

'I saw him at some of those – parties. I had nothing to do with him, of course. He was just there . . . a sort of part of it. Then I didn't see him again until I came to live at Hawley House – I'd forgotten all about him, that people like that even existed. But he . . . contacted me, I suppose you'd call it. I'd been doing some shopping in Illingford . . . suddenly he was sitting there at the table with me, in Derry's, in the Coffee Garden. It was like a nightmare. I was on my own; I looked up, and there he sat.'

'Why didn't you walk out?' Gently said.

'I couldn't do that . . . he had an effect on me. I seemed to know in a moment that he had some power over me. He said he'd met an old flame of mine, the one who used to take me to parties, and did I think he should be discreet about that or did my in-laws know already. What could I possibly say to him? He had an effect that was simply mesmeric. You found yourself saying and doing anything just to break the spell, to get rid of him.

'He asked for a loan of fifty pounds and I opened my handbag and paid it to him. He said at the end of the month he might be short, and could he rely on my generosity? He wrote an address on a slip of paper. I could send it there, he said – the same sum, unregistered, on the last day of each month. Then I was sure he would stay my friend, that he would always protect my reputation.

'And suddenly his chair was empty again. And I burst into tears. I couldn't help it . . .'

Hastings reached out to press her hand.

'It's all right, Dave,' she said. 'Don't fuss me.'

'By God, I'd have maimed him!' Hastings said. 'It was just after I'd paid him to keep away from you.'

'Dave, you mustn't talk like that.'

Hastings looked fiercely at Gently. 'Now you've a picture of him,' he said. 'This is the man you're making trouble over.'

Gently nodded. 'Point taken! Perhaps now we can come to something more important?'

'What's more important?'

'Shall we say – the state of the market, when Shimpling smelled a divorce in the offing?'

Laura Buxhall's hand went to her mouth.

'Steady, Lolly!' Hastings said. 'The Superintendent is good at guessing. That's what superintendents are for.'

'I'm not guessing,' Gently said. 'Just dealing the cards off the pack. Shimpling wouldn't have missed a trick like that, especially when it was to lose him a couple of clients. If that divorce had gone through he would have lost his hold on you for good – so he had either to bust the divorce, or settle for a lump-sum payment. But he couldn't easily bust the divorce without prejudicing his set-up, so he chose the lump sum. Isn't that a logical sequence?'

'Lolly, don't say anything,' Hastings said.

'He must have asked plenty,' Gently said. 'Dr Cheyne-Chevington had private resources, Lady

166

Buxhall a millionaire husband. And this was the pay-off, the once-for-all. I'd say Shimpling was asking five figures. Maybe twenty . . . thirty thousand: he'd certainly open his mouth wide.'

'Go on – have fun!' Hastings snapped.

'Only this time he opened it too wide. Usually he didn't make mistakes like that, but just this once he'd priced himself out. You couldn't or you wouldn't pay him. On the other hand you couldn't and wouldn't do nothing. So how was this interesting plot to end? What were the final cards to be?'

'You know I have an alibi!' Hastings exclaimed.

Gently shook his head. 'I know you haven't. Groton is the only one with an alibi – unless Sayers comes up with something convincing.'

'I was right here – in this chalet.'

'Part of the night you may have been.'

'Ask Cockfield. Ask Ashfield—'

'Perhaps I should ask Lady Buxhall?'

'I – what should I know about it?' Laura Buxhall faltered. 'I wasn't anywhere . . . I didn't know any-thing!'

'You weren't told what was going to happen?'

'No . . . nothing about the tiger.'

'Lolly,' David Hastings shouted.

'I'm sorry, I'm sorry!' she cried in confusion. 'I can't tell you anything, I don't know anything. David, get me out of here . . . I want to go!'

She jumped to her feet. Hastings, gone pale, followed her through the doors with the bottle-glass insets. Only moments later an engine started and car wheels crunched on the gravelled drive. Hastings came back. He stood haggardly by the doors, face thinned, lips tight. Gently had got out his pipe and was stolidly filling it. On the floor lay Laura Bughall's glass.

Hastings came forward. 'Well?' he asked dully.

Gently struck a match. 'Give me Sayers,' he said.

'Sayers?'

'For him, I'll keep Lady Laura out of it. You know she wouldn't stand up for five minutes.'

'But I can't do that!'

'Please yourself. You wanted a deal, I'm giving you one.'

'But Sayers—'

'Where is he?'

David Hastings bit his lips.

Gently rose, puffing smoke. He said to Dutt:

'Come on!'

CHAPTER FOURTEEN

B Y A MIRACLE – or was it because people were
beginning to know Gently? – he and Dutt were
left to eat their lunch at the Angel in peace.

It was Saturday menu, no doubt concocted with an
eye on the farmers. It included roast turkey, roast
chicken, roast sirloin and beef pudding.

The sweets were also more substantial; special today
was an apple dumpling, huge servings of which,
swimming in thick custard, kept going past to the
tables. It was Dutt's choice. The Saturday menu was
clearly earning his approval. Before the apple dumpling
he had silently tucked away what looked like a quarter
of a good-sized turkey.

Then dreamily over the coffee he remarked:

'These country boys know how to eat!'

And for a while he sat sleepily, benignly watching
the dispatch of food by other customers.

Gently had fared more abstemiously, on chicken
followed by fruit salad. He'd looked wistfully at Dutt's
apple dumpling, but had been warned by a lingering
soreness in his head . . .

'Is that the chemist bloke over there, chief?'

Gently looked where Dutt was indicating. Yes, it was Ashfield all right, at a corner table at the end of the room. He must just have arrived; his black head was bobbing over a plate of vegetable soup. Opposite him sat his grey-haired wife with a glass of tomato juice before her.

'Can't say I admire his taste . . .'

As though she'd heard, Mrs Ashfield stared towards them. A stare of hard, penetrating condemnation. Then she spoke to Ashfield, but he didn't turn round.

'Blimey!' Dutt said.

Gently shrugged feebly. 'For all you know, she's an excellent woman.'

'That's just what I mean, chief – she's an excellent woman.'

'Perhaps that's the reason why he's a philosopher.'

But perhaps he loved his wife too? Gently watched the black head from the corner of his eye. Ashfield wasn't a timid man, either, he'd fire up soon enough if you roused him. Yet he submitted to those ugly assistants, and shrank from a showdown about Shirley Banks . . . was it fear? Was it love? Possibly a mixture of both.

'Anyway, don't leave Ashfield out of your reckoning.'

'Don't worry, chief, I wasn't going to.'

'Keep pressuring him, Cockfield and Hastings. Keep an eye on Groton. Find the other two.'

'Especially the other two,' Dutt said. 'What line shall I take with Lady Laura?'

'She's your ace in the hole. She'll break down easily. But don't make use of her unless you have to.'

Because, in any case, how much did she know? Most likely she'd told the truth about that! It was possible that until a few days ago she'd never known how the blackmailer had been dealt with. Hastings would have said: 'We're going to have a showdown – Shimpling won't threaten us any more.' And so it had been: all she could tell them was that Hastings was implicated, and perhaps with whom.

Whereas what they wanted so much to know . . . but nothing fresh had come in on Banks or Sayers.

'Banks can prove the blackmail set-up. Get it out of her somehow! Once it's proved you can squeeze the others, make it really fierce for them. They must know where Sayers is hiding. Hastings knows for a certainty. And that's how you'll use Lady Laura – as a jemmy to prize open Hastings.

'Meanwhile, keep them checking on Hastings. He probably forged documents when he switched identities.'

'I'll do my best, chief,' Dutt said.

Gently grinned. 'You'll manage,' he said. 'Keep up the pressure, that's all. These people aren't pros. They'll crack.'

But he sighed, lighting his after-lunch pipe. Really oughtn't he to stay with it for another day . . . say over the weekend, by which time Miss Banks must surely be in the bag?

That's what the Assistant Commissioner would have envisaged, Gently getting his teeth in and staying

171

on . . . leaving Evans to loiter by his side with nobody to use his spare rod. Yes, that was the idea! When had Gently ever left a case unfinished?

Right now, as he set off to drive to his golf club, the AC would be chuckling over his astuteness . . .

'Superintendent Gently, sir?'

A waiter stood by them.

Gently volleyed smoke. 'Who wants me?'

'On the phone, sir. Gave the name of Barnes. Said it was very urgent he should speak to you.'

Gently grunted pessimistically, but got up and followed the waiter. The waiter led him into the office, where a phone lay off its cradle. Gently took it.

'Gently here . . .'

'Chiefie, you've got to get out to Groton's place!'

'What is it – a fire?'

'No, this is serious! Grab some men and get out here.'

Gently settled slowly on the desktop. 'Now,' he said, 'in words of one syllable. Why should a chief superintendent leave his lunch and rush anywhere on the say-so of a crime reporter?'

'I'll tell you why,' Barnes gabbled. 'There's a panther loose, for one thing! And there's a blonde up a tree taking pot-shots at it – and Groton taking pot-shots at everyone else! For crying out loud, chiefie, it isn't a leg-pull.

'Bring some men – and bring guns!'

It wasn't a leg-pull.

The lane to Groton's farm was jammed with cars

when Gently arrived. Swearing, he had to park with two wheels in a ditch, a hundred yards from the farm gate.

As he and Dutt alighted a shotgun cracked and shot swished overhead. It pattered harmlessly into the hedge, but it had people shouting and diving behind cars.

Barnes ran up.

'Have you brought some men?'

'They're on their way. What are these people doing?'

'Stupid bloody rubbernecks! I've been trying to tell them – Groton is threatening to let out the animals—'

'Where's this panther?'

'Sitting under the tree. She's emptied her gun and never scratched it!'

Men, women, even two children hung about the cars jamming the lane. A photographer was lying on top of a shooting-brake, taking shot after shot with a Leica. In an upper window of the farmhouse Groton was visible. You could see the gun lying in the crook of his arm.

'How did the woman get here?'

'Drove up in that Anglia. Marched up to the farmhouse as bold as brass! When Groton opened the door she pulled a gun on him – just stuck it straight into his guts.'

'Then?'

'They went inside. The boys were flabbergasted – couldn't believe it. Some of them wanted to ring you, the others thought they'd hang on.'

173

'So, of course, nobody rang.'

'Oh, chiefie, we're all human! This was the crime scoop of the decade – cameras, everything at the ready. And we'd earned it. All day we'd been here with Groton pumping lead at us—'

'Who let the panther out?'

'Groton. At least—'

'Don't tell me! You didn't see him.'

He marched on up the lane, deliberately shoving people aside. Near the farm gate a covey of pressmen were deployed behind a fence. Groton had seen Gently. He threw his gun up and aimed at him. Gently kept on walking. Groton didn't fire.

Nearer the gate one could hear the animal noises coming from the cages behind the outbuilding. At the corner of the outbuilding a cameraman was crouched: only his head projected farther.

'Fsst! The panther's just round there.'

Gently stopped by the pressmen.

'Did anyone see what happened?'

'We couldn't, chiefie. It happened at the back.'

'Well?'

'The bird was screaming her head off. We belted down here and round the buildings. There's a paddock back there with a thorn-tree in it. She was going up the tree like a jack-in-a-box. Then we saw the panther go loping across and start circling round the tree, and the bird was screeching and popping off at it and clawing higher up into the branches.'

'So what did you do?'

'What the hell could we do? We grabbed some

quick pics and scapa'd! She's all right if she stays put. He'll never make it into the thorn tree.'

'Brave boys,' Gently said. 'Where was Groton this while?'

'Didn't see him. The next we knew he was shooting and shouting out of his window.'

'Stay here,' Gently said to Dutt.

He went along to the crouching cameraman. He touched the man's shoulder. The man jumped.

'Move back,' Gently said. 'Let me look.'

From the corner of the outhouse he could see the two compounds and the paddock behind them and the thorn tree. It was a large thorn tree which had been browsed by cattle and presented a flat base of tangled boughs. In the top of the tree clung the woman. Her clothing was torn and she was bleeding. She was half-hanging, half-clinging, head drawn back, eyes fixed below. And underneath sat the panther, very still, staring up.

'He's had a go at the tree . . . it's the thorns, they've got him puzzled.'

'What do you do if he comes this way?'

'Run like a bastard for that car.'

'No pics?'

'No pics. And no bloody camera. Just me.'

Gently patted his arm. 'You've got the idea. You stay here and keep an eye on him.'

He moved back to the huddle of reporters. Almost immediately some shot whined over. It was aimed low and scythed through a hedge-top, leaving frayed twigs showing white.

Gently called: 'Groton!'

Groton bellowed with laughter. He fired a second barrel, this time high.

'He says he'll open the cages,' somebody muttered. 'There's a puma in there and a couple of wolves.'

'Groton!' Gently called. 'What are you trying to prove? Come out and help us catch the panther!'

'You take a jump at yourself!' Groton bawled. 'I didn't ask you lot to come around.'

'Groton, there's a woman in danger back there.'

'So what? I didn't invite her either.'

'If anything happens to her, you'll be to blame.'

'Like hell! She drew on me – haven't you heard?'

'Groton, I'm ordering you to come out.'

Groton laughed and fired in the air.

'He sounds a bit loco, chief,' Dutt said.

A reporter said: 'He's been loco all day.'

'Who's in there with him?' Gently asked.

'Nobody. His help knocked off at lunchtime.'

Then Perkins dashed up, his face drooping with wretchedness. He was so agitated that he could only mow and gasp for some seconds. Then he blurted:

'Is it true . . . about the lion, I mean?'

'It's a panther.'

'Oh . . . a panther.'

'It's in the paddock round the back.'

'But it's loose, is it . . . and the woman . . . ?'

The reporters were staring at him curiously. Nobody could take Perkins seriously! Yet you couldn't doubt his sincerity.

'Have you brought a rifle?'

'Yes. They rushed it over from the barracks. Asked if we needed a marksman . . . but Bulley . . . you remember?'

'He's the one who shot the tiger.'

'Yes . . . he's very cool . . . a police medal . . .'

'Bring him up here. Groton won't help us. I'm afraid we'll have to shoot the brute.'

Perkins turned and waved dramatically. Constable Bulley came up at the double. He was carrying the rifle rather gingerly and wore an expression of quiet tenseness. Gently nodded to the rifle.

'You've checked that, Bulley – you're ready to go?'

Bulley swallowed and nodded back.

'Six in the breech, sir . . . one up the spout.'

'Then for the love of God put the catch on!'

Bulley put on the catch.

'Follow me. The rest keep back – if you've any sense, you'll get in the cars.'

He led the way to the corner of the outbuilding, round which the cameraman had now poked his instrument. The scene, the woman in the tree, the panther below her, had changed only in one particular.

'You'd better be quick – I think she's all in. And that cunning bastard seems to know it . . .'

The woman had slid a little lower in the thorn tree and her head had drooped forward.

Gently glanced at Bulley.

'Will you risk it from here . . . ?'

'Well, I don't know, sir . . .'

'I think we'll go forward. If we can crawl to that hedge you'll get an easy shot. It's a cross-wind – he shouldn't smell us.'

'What about me?' the cameraman whispered.

'If you move from here I'll have your ticket!'

They set off crawling, first over pocked mud rolled iron-hard by the passage of vehicles, then across a rough concrete hard-standing, then on to coarse grass mixed with plantain and docks. Behind them they could hear Groton roaring and the reports of his shotgun. In front they could see only the hedge and, above it, the woman hung in the tree.

They reached the hedge. It was tall and spindly, composed of Marabella plum. At its foot was a tangle of grasses, nettles and the dead stems of hogweed.

'Work along it!' Gently whispered. 'If we push into this stuff he'll hear us. There's a bit of a gap . . .'

Bulley followed him doggedly, with the rifle grasped across its breech.

'Now . . . there he is!'

They'd come to a gap which had perhaps been opened by rabbits. Through it, at a distance of thirty yards, they could see the panther squatted by the tree. He was looking upwards very intently, and the twitch of his snowy whiskers was visible. The corner of his mouth was dragged open and had saliva descending from it.

As they watched, Groton fired his gun. The panther slicked its ears but didn't turn.

'Behind the shoulder . . . below the spine.'

There was a desperation about Bulley. He seemed unable to get his elbows planted and the butt was loose against his shoulder. Then he was forgetting that catch again! It was Gently who reached over and tipped it off.

'Now – give it to him!'

Bulley yanked, and the muzzle rose above a foot.

'Let me have it!' Gently bawled.

The panther was snarling and leaping backwards. A wicket's length beyond the tree it stopped in a crouch, its tail swishing.

Gently scrambled up, keeping his eye on the panther, working the bolt of the rifle by feel. Now it was a far more difficult shot – what did one aim at, from the front?

Perhaps through the mouth . . .

He froze round the rifle, jogging his feet firm apart. The panther had seen him through the screen of the fence and was stalking towards him, belly to the ground.

Between the eyes? Would that find the spine?

He centred the pip an inch lower. Then he pressed, felt the jar cushion in him, saw the silver belly of the beast rise in front of him.

'By crikey . . . he's bought it!'

The panther was thrashing on its side, trying to dig its head into the ground.

It was giving pathetic snarling yelps as though incredulous of its mortal agony.

Then, very suddenly, it jerked still.

Blood began to pool by its muzzle.

'You got him!'

Bulley couldn't believe it. He was trembling all over, his eyes were staring.

Gently shoved the rifle at him.

'Here!' he said. 'You're the man with the medal.'

The double crack of the rifle brought people running. Just then they seemed to have forgotten about Groton. The photographer who'd been scouting was first on the spot, and he took a fine picture of Bulley juggling with the rifle.

In fact, it was a problem what to photograph first! The panther had kindly died in a dramatic posture. In her tree, though out of danger, the woman persisted in hanging on, apparently determined to give the cameras a chance.

Then there was Gently, always a safe subject, striding over to the tree and talking up to her.

And if that wasn't enough, it seemed likely she was going to faint . . .

'Dutt, get up there and bring her down.'

More fodder for the cameras!

Swearing under his breath about the thorns, Dutt eased her down in slow lifts.

She was a blonde of about thirty-five. When you saw her close her face looked mean. Her black dress was ripped in the skirt and her stockings were ripped and burst at the knees. Blood from the thorn wounds was congealing on her legs, arms, neck.

She said huskily: 'Glad you made it, boys,' keeping tight hold of Dutt's arm.

Under the tree lay an automatic, a .22 Browning, a mere gimcrack.

'Is that your gun?' Gently asked.

She looked at him sideways. 'Yeah,' she said.

'Are these your shoes?'

'I kicked them off. Looks like he tried one for flavour.'

'Is your name Shirley Banks?'

'Yeah,' she said. And fainted.

'All right!' Gently said. 'Get back, everyone. This is police business, not a press stunt.'

'That's where you're wrong, feller,' a voice said.

Behind them stood Groton, with a revolver,

The revolver was a Colt .45 but it didn't look so big in Groton's hand. He wasn't pointing it at them particularly, it was just hanging in their direction.

'Yes, you're wrong, feller,' Groton repeated. 'As from now on, this is my business. And what I'm telling you, one and all, is to get to hell out of my kraal!'

Gently said: 'Put that gun away, Groton.'

Groton chucked his massive head. 'Not just for you telling me, copper,' he said. 'I don't like coppers who shoot my cats.'

'I'm arresting you, Groton.'

Groton laughed. 'That'll be the day, copper,' he said. 'But just now you're marching out through that gate. You're a bloody trespasser, and I don't stand for them.'

'You just set panthers on them,' Gently said.

'If they poke a gun at me,' Groton said. 'Or maybe I pick them up with one hand and toss them clear back to the road. It's up to me, how I deal with trespassers. There's boards warning them to keep out. All you need to know is what I'm telling you — collect your riff-raff and hop it!'

He made a waving motion with the Colt and some of the pressmen drew back involuntarily. Groton snorted his scorn, spun the Colt by its trigger-guard.

Would he really use the gun? They weren't close enough to rush him . . .

Yet if they called his bluff and stayed put, how was that going to end?

Then, strangely, the moment found its man. Perkins went stalking out towards Grown. The move was so unexpected that even Groton's eyes widened.

'What do you want, Perky?'

'Give me your gun. I'm arresting you, Groton.'

'You're doing what?'

'Arresting you. Give me the gun and come quietly.'

It was absurd! Perkins stood nearly a head shorter than Groton – he was half the man; yet there he waited, hand out-stretched for the revolver. Groton stared for a moment, then bellowed with laughter.

'You're a comic, Perky!' he roared. 'You'd better go home and play with the kiddoes – us nasty big boys might make you cry.'

'Are you giving it me?'

'Go chase your tail, Perky.'

'Groton, I want that gun.'

'Don't upset me, little man. I might sneeze and knock you down.'

What happened next was rather confused. Presumably Perkins tried to grab the gun. Groton roared and aimed a blow at Perkins which should have taken his head off his shoulders.

But . . . it didn't! Instead, Perkins grabbed him and

made a knee in a deft manner. And Groton flew. The whole colossal bulk of him up-ended and crashed headlong.

'Go – get him!' Gently shouted.

Bulley, Hargrave rushed to help Perkins.

But Groton was out. He'd gone down on his head. Perkins had floored him with one throw!

And, most amazing of all, now it was done Perkins seemed completely shamefaced. He picked up the revolver and brought it to Gently with the air of a dog who expects a whipping.

'I'm sorry . . . I didn't want to use violence . . .'

Was there any limit to the man?

'I mean, our reputation . . . that Sheffield business . . .'

'Who taught you judo?'

'Well . . . Sayers.'

Then he was being mobbed by the pressmen, who were climbing over each other with their cameras – who had a personal score against Groton, and had suddenly found themselves a hero . . .

Fantastic!

In the background, Groton was sitting up bemusedly. They'd forced some handcuffs on his mighty wrists and he was stupidly jangling them together. Then they heaved him to his feet, and he stood rubber-kneed, wavering.

'The lady's coming round, chief.'

The lady? She was old news already.

But all this while Dutt had tended her impassively, kneeling by her, chafing her hands. Now she moaned and her eyes came open.

'Take it easy, miss!' Dutt said.

She looked at him. 'Gawd!' she said. 'I feel like death. What's going on?'

'You're all right, miss.'

'You kidding, man? I couldn't unpop my suspenders.'

'We'll run you to the hospital in a minute, miss.'

'I'd sooner you ran me to a boozer.'

Her eyes sharpened.

'That bastard,' she said. 'Where is he – what have you done with him?'

'Groton, miss? He's under arrest.'

'Help me up. Let me look at him!'

Dutt glanced at Gently. Gently nodded. Dutt slipped an arm under her and lifted. Hanging on his arm, she was able to take a few steps to where she could see the animal dealer. She stared her hate at him.

'The murderous swine. He did for Peter – you know that?'

'Peter Shimpling . . . ?'

'You don't know yet? You bloody coppers don't know anything.'

'Have you proof of this, Miss Banks?'

'I saw the letter, I can swear to that. Of course he pinched it back again, but—'

Her eyes jumped wide. Groton had seen her. Dutt could feel her fingers hook into his arm. Groton's deepset eyes were blazing animal-like, like the blind staring of one of his cats.

And suddenly he roared, heaved against his chest, sent the handcuffs flying from his wrists . . .

'Pull him down!'

There wasn't time! His right hand snatched, drew back, whirled. Something flew, landed with a thump, and Shirley Banks collapsed screaming.

CHAPTER FIFTEEN

THE AMBULANCE ARRIVED.

Shirley Banks hadn't been seriously wounded by Groton's knife. It had struck her high up in the left shoulder and had glanced upwards over the bone.

But she had bled a lot and was in great pain, and went out like a light when she got a jab.

If Groton's intention had been to stop her talking, for the moment he had succeeded.

After throwing the knife he'd tried to make a break for it, running in the direction of his vehicles. But about twenty of them, police and pressmen, had chased after him and brought him down. He'd been roughed-up in the melee and was now no advertisement for restrained handling. This time he was handcuffed behind his back and also pinioned with a length of lighting-flex.

Then he was hustled to a car, in another camera-festival, and driven off to the cells.

From the time he'd been disarmed and thrown by Perkins he hadn't spoken one word.

When the car had left Perkins sought out Gently.

'What can we do about the animals . . .?'

Poor fellow! He was quite thrown out of his stride by the lionizing of the pressmen. He hung about, looking a picture of guilt, trying hard to keep himself in the background. Evidently he couldn't forget that terrible moment when he'd used violence to effect an arrest . . .

'We'd better call in his hired help. They should know what to do.'

'But Groton did the feeding, don't you remember?'

'All right. Try the RSPCA.'

'But would they know . . .'

'Just try them!'

Perkins began to look happier. Irritating people he understood, it put him on better terms with himself.

'Also, you'd better get a search warrant. You might turn up something in the house.'

'We only have the woman's word for it . . .'

'Come on. I want to see Groton's car.'

He strode off towards the compound, with the menage hurrying after him. But somehow, now that Groton and Shirley Banks had gone, one could feel an atmosphere of anticlimax.

The stars were missing . . . Nobody quite knew what the drama they had played portended, but it had been an enthralling drama, proceeding with an inner logic of its own.

All that was left now was the set and a few of the props, like the dead panther.

'Which of you is Slater?'

'I'm Slater.'

He was the cameraman who'd lurked at the corner.

'I want you to look at Groton's estate car, to see if anything's changed since you took your photograph.'

They examined the car. The off-side headlamp had no glass and was dented. The fairing below it was also dented and the glass of the sidelight cracked. Part of the grille was driven in and the horn and end of the bumper bent.

'Anything altered?'

'He's cleared the glass out. A lot of it was there when I took the pic.'

'Who else could have got at the car today?'

'Well, his two men were here this morning.'

'Nobody else?'

'His housekeeper. He's had no visitors – apart from the blonde.'

A pressman asked: 'What do you make of it, chiefie?'

Gently shrugged. 'You can see what I see. Groton took his car out last night and collided with something – or somebody.'

'Can we print the "somebody"?'

'After we've checked. Haven't you enough stuff for one day?'

Aside to Perkins he said: 'Have the car brought in. And when you're searching here – find that glass!'

But the sense of anticlimax persisted . . . what was a hit-and-run case, after all? Every day people died on the roads, it was strictly commonplace, non-news.

More to the point was the chewed shoe which Dutt, perhaps unconsciously, was carrying about with him, or the question which Perkins was dying to ask but daren't:

'What ought we to do with the panther?'

Anticlimax! The point where routine took over from sensation.

'Leave a man here, and let's get back. Maybe Groton will have found his tongue.'

A sad-faced constable named Culford was selected to stand guard. The pressmen scattered to their cars, suddenly silent and urgent. Hargrave, putting on a big act, was dispersing sightseers from the lane.

Then a squad car arrived. Gipping jumped out, looking excited.

'The Yard have rung us, sir . . . it's rather peculiar. I thought you should know straight away.'

'What's bothering them?'

'Shimpling, sir. They've identified another man as Shimpling.'

'Another man?'

'Yes, sir. He's dead. He was killed in an accident last night. There was identification on the body.'

Gently stared. 'Let's get this straight! He's been identified as our Shimpling?'

'Yes, sir. Living at a flat in Fulham, just off the King's Road.'

'Killed in an accident?'

'In Kingsway, sir. He was stepping off the pavement when he was hit. They're trying to find the car now, but they're sure it's the same Shimpling.'

Gently looked at Perkins. Perkins had turned red. One could read his thoughts as though they were being screened on that quickly sagging, chubby face.

'But that's nonsense!'

Gently shook his head. On the contrary, it was perfect sense.

'But then . . . who's the one we've got in the morgue?'

'Who else is missing?'

Perkins gaped.

Groton wasn't talking.

He sat in his cell with the broody withdrawal of a penned gorilla, deaf, ignoring all about him, alive only in his smouldering eyes.

Perkins read out the charge to him – intent to murder and actual GBH – but the formal warning that Groton need say nothing must have sounded ridiculous even to Perkins.

Groton hadn't, wasn't saying anything.

He needed no warning, now or ever.

When Perkins had finished Groton climbed on the bunk, turned his face to the wall, apparently slept.

But if Groton was saying nothing, Shirley Banks wanted to say plenty. Only two hours after she was admitted to hospital the telephone rang.

'This is Abbotsham District Hospital, Sister Brassey, Emergency Ward . . .'

The patient Banks was being difficult and demanded to talk to Superintendent Gently.

'Is she fit to talk?' Gently asked.

'Perfectly fit, in her opinion. But she won't calm down until she's seen you, so you may as well visit her.'

Gently, Perkins, Dutt, drove to the hospital. Shirley Banks was in a private room. She was lying propped up on a white-painted iron bedstead and had on a hospital shift of coarse linen.

'Don't tell me – I'm looking a fright!'

In point of fact, she merely looked like a patient. Her face had been scrubbed of its thick cosmetics and her hair brushed cleanly back and pinned. She had patches of plaster on her neck and arms, a dressing taped to her left shoulder.

Without the cosmetics she looked older, pleasanter. Her eyes were woosey from the injection.

'Sit down . . . have you brought a notebook with you? Hell! This shoulder's giving me socks . . .

'Do you really feel up to it, Miss Banks?'

'Sit down, copper. I'm the boss round here.'

Gently sat in a comfortless easy chair. Dutt took out his notebook and perched on the radiator.

The room was small and seemed to lack something. What was missing? Yes – flowers!

'Where do I start? You know about Peter?'

Gently nodded. 'We've heard.'

'Copper, you nail Groton for that good and proper. He's a murderous bastard from his heels up.'

'You mentioned a letter . . .'

'Yes, the letter. He pinched it back along with the other stuff. He'd jemmied the door and frisked the place . . . a damn fine mess the bastard made.'

'What was in the letter?'

'It fixed the appointment, nine-thirty at Groton's club. Anywhere else Pete wouldn't have gone – he knew the swine too well for that.

'But the Safari Club, that was different. What could Groton pull there?'

'Why did he want to meet Groton?'

'Don't kid me, copper. It was a bit of black. All this time Pete was lying low . . . then the body turned up. It did something to him. Mind you, he'd never been the same, not like he was before it happened. But the body turning up made him snap out of it – made him angry, I guess that was it.

'So he sent a black-letter to Groton and Groton made the appointment. A couple of thou he should have brought. But all Pete got was a car in the back.'

'And you came up here . . . ?'

Her lids dropped.

'Yeah, I came up here because I was mad. Because I wanted to make him pay. I wouldn't have cared a crap if I'd shot him.

'You know what he told me? That the panther was his banker, that he kept his dough in its cage. And I swallowed it, a line like that. Next thing I was clawing up a tree.'

She gave a shudder, then fell swearing at the pain in her shoulder.

'Now I know what it's like,' she said. 'I can understand what it did to Peter.'

'What did it do to Peter?'

She moaned, touched the dressing with a finger.

'His hair went white, that's the spitting truth. Two days afterwards he was white.'

'After what?'

'After what happened. He couldn't get out of that bloody place. He had to listen to it eating the bloke . . . it gave him the screaming willies for months.'

'We're talking about the tiger?'

'What the hell else?'

'I'd like you to tell me what happened before that.'

She slid a look at him.

'Are you pinching me, copper?'

Gently shook his head.

'Yeah,' she said. 'Well, OK.'

She reached for the water-container on her locker, but Perkins was there first. He slopped water in her glass. She ran a casual eye over Perkins.

'Man,' she said, 'don't blush for those shoulders!'

Perkins retired. Miss Banks drank water.

'So about Peter and me,' she said. 'We were buddies from a long time back – maybe I don't have to tell you about that. Pete was a nance. That didn't bother me, we had our moments, all the same. He was nice to me, always nice. That goes a long way with a girl.

'Then we did a little work together . . . he could trust me, understand? Mostly blacks work on their own, but Pete and me made a team. He'd give me a mark and I'd lay him, Pete would be there with the camera. Sometimes he pulled a nance job and then it was me who took the picture. I got a percentage. He never gyped me. I haven't been on the bash for years. I used to pick up the dough for him mostly – clients were forgetful about posting it.

'Pete got his hooks into the doctor, but he lost him for a time after the trial. That made him mad because the doctor had roughed him up, and there was a fat connection Pete was after. Pete had a screw on Groton too. That bastard had killed some natives in Kenya. Pete had a picture of him with the bodies and a truck behind them, showing the number plate. Groton whipped that, of course. He cleaned out everything from the flat.

'Anyway, when Pete was in Abbotsham collecting money from Groton he met the doctor again – he was living here under a different name. That gave Pete a notion to come here. He was having a bit of trouble in town. One of his clients had swallowed a gun and I don't know, one thing and another. Anyway, the doctor was flogging houses and Pete blacked him for a bungalow, then we moved in and started building a connection out this way.

'Pete was good, you know that? He was a bloody fine operator. He could smell black in a moment and he could handle clients when he got them. Once he read a case in the paper – didn't know a thing about the bloke! – but he sat down and wrote this fellow a letter, and next day I was collecting the moolah.

'Laugh? We killed ourselves over that one! He'd a sense of humour, Pete had.'

'Was the name of that client Edward Cockfield?'

Shirley Banks said: 'I don't remember.'

'Yes, you do,' Gently said. 'If I'm not pinching you, I want names.'

She pouted. 'You're a right copper! All right, it was Cockfield. So what?'

'Just give me the names – all ten of them.'

She slanted a look at him, muttered something.

'So there was Groton and this fellow – and the doctor, you'd know about him. Then there was Lady Buxhall, the doctor's girlfriend, just a tart who'd married rich. And Bert Drinkstone, he's a magistrate – got a taste for being flogged. And the chemist – he was a lark! – and Joe Leyton who runs the Majestic.

'Then there was Sayers, he was a nance job, and Gwen Eliegh and Gertie Wratting. Those perishing women were oonch-fanciers.

'What are you blushing about, feller?'

Perkins said agitatedly: 'She must be lying! I know those ladies very well . . . Mrs Wratting in particular. She's honorary president of the Dining Club.'

Shirley Banks gave a gritty chuckle. 'Where have you been hiding, sonny?' she asked.

'She's a public figure—!'

'She's a randy old bitch. Pete had to come in and drag her away from me.'

'And Miss Eliegh is chairman—'

'She gave me a pain. You'd laugh if I told you what her game is.'

'You can't believe what this woman is saying . . . Mr Drinkstone too. It's unthinkable!'

Gently sighed, hunched weary shoulders. Perhaps he should have left Perkins out of it! Somewhere, in any statement by Shirley Banks, fresh Abbotsham heads were going to roll . . .

'Right,' he said. 'That'll do, Miss Banks.'

'Man, I'll give details if he wants them.'

'Get back to the statement.'

She leered at Perkins. Perkins turned his back, stood twisting his fingers.

'So that was Pete's connection here,' Miss Banks said. 'We were running it about a year. Pete knew how to keep them cool, nobody made him any trouble. Then something happened that put a scare in me. I spotted a bloke on my tail. He was checking who I spoke to, where I was picking up the envelopes.'

'What did he look like?'

'A real creep. I didn't reckon him for a cop. I saw him around a couple of days before I figured what his game was.'

'Could he have been a private detective?'

'That's what Pete and me thought. Pete was trying for a big dip just then, he reckoned he'd stirred up some opposition.'

'What did you do?'

'I wanted to leave – but not Pete. Pete had guts. He reckoned they wouldn't dare touch him · if they couldn't get hold of the stuff. So we arranged it I went back to London and took the stuff along with me. Then after he'd made his big dip he'd join me there, then we'd work the connection by mail.

'Two months later he turned up at Fulham at around two in the morning. He was shaking and blubbing like an idiot, and all he could say to me was "the tiger!"'

Shirley Banks laid her head back.

'Now I know how he felt,' she said. 'Maybe I didn't right then, but I do now. Poor bastard.'

'But he told you what happened,' Gently said.

'Yeah,' she said. 'I got it out of him. Not right away. He was shot to bits. Later on I heard the details.

'Somebody came knocking on his door. He wasn't expecting any callers. He took a poker down the hall, opened the door and let fly. Then everything happened. A truck backed up. He could see the tiger in the truck. He could see the grille going up. He dived into the bathroom and locked the door.

'And that's where he had to stay, listening to the tiger noshing the bloke. He couldn't leave through the window because it was a bloody silly window. When it was quiet he peeked out and all he could see was the tiger's leavings. He belted across to the garage, got in the car, got to hell.

'That's about it — except he woke up screaming every night for six months.'

'And the bloke he hit?' Gently asked.

'He never saw who it was. The bloke rushed him when he opened the door, he clocked him one, the bloke went down.'

Gently slowly nodded his head. Yes . . . the details all fitted. Even the missing car, and the burial of the remains which were perhaps not beyond identification. But who had been driving Groton's truck, who had winched up that grille? Who had come back later, while the tiger still roamed, to dig the grave and remove evidence?

Groton knew, no doubt of that. But Groton wasn't saying a word.

Shirley Banks was watching him anxiously.

'Have I told you too much, copper?' she asked.

Gently shrugged. 'You know what you've told me! But proving it is different. I wouldn't worry.'

'I'd do a stretch to fix Groton. The pity of it is they won't hang him.'

'You'd better relax.' Gently climbed to his feet. 'We'll bring you something to sign later.'

'Not nothing incriminating I won't sign!'

'Nothing incriminating.'

Gently smiled at her.

They drove back to Headquarters. Nothing was said in the car. The crowd from the football had turned out and they were jammed for ten minutes in Abbeygate Street.

In Perkins's office Gently lit his pipe and stood some moments gazing at the window. Perkins, equally absorbed, lumped down at his desk, and appeared to read doom in the marks on his blotter.

Only Dutt, beginning to type from his notes, seemed exempt from this impulse to silence.

At last Gently turned.

He said: 'Here's the problem! We're in a rather unusual situation. We have to decide whether to declare or to keep playing till stumps.'

Perkins blurted: 'We can't go on . . . can't bring all those people into it.'

'We might keep it down to one or two.'

198

'No . . . you don't know Abbotsham. It'd come out!'

'Then let's take a look at the situation.' Gently gave several quick puffs. 'Fast, Groton. He's off your hands. He'll go to London. You can forget him. Then there's a murder that isn't a murder but an accidental death – a death resulting from the commission of a felony by the deceased and others unknown. Along with which you have a lesser crime, that of concealing the death.

'Now, do we send it to the coroner like that, on the hard evidence we can offer, or do we ask for another postponement and try to identify the others un-known?'

Perkins groaned. 'We know who they were.'

Gently shook his head. 'That won't do. All we can show is that certain people acted suspiciously, and that a prostitute claims they had a motive. On that evidence we couldn't proceed. The Public Prosecutor wouldn't accept it. But we could go on probing and pressuring these people on the chance of getting a confession.'

He blew a heavy gust of smoke.

'What it really amounts to is this! If I take myself off and go fishing, you can settle this according to Abbotsham.'

'What . . . what . . . ?'

Perkins's eyes rolled incredulously.

'Of course, I'm not putting ideas into your head. But if you said to me these people have suffered enough already, I should probably have to agree with you.

'They've broken the law, but they've paid for it. Isn't that all that justice requires? No point in making them pay twice, and wasting public money into the bargain. Better let them go on being good citizens.

'Well – I couldn't argue against that!'

'B-but . . .' Perkins stammered.

'It just leaves two things,' Gently said. 'One of them is personal curiosity. The other is what happened to Sayers's money, if indeed it was Sayers the tiger ate. You'd agree with that, would you? We ought to know?'

'Y-yes . . . but . . .'

'Hand me the phone. If I make an early start tomorrow I can be in Wales by teatime.'

A gaping Perkins pushed the phone across. Gently lifted it and dialled.

'Cockfield? . . . Superintendent Gently. I'd like you to invite me out this evening.'

'You'd like me to do what?' Cockfield said.

'Invite me out to your chalet. With Hastings and Ashfield. Just the four of us. I thought you'd prefer it on your own ground.'

A moment's silence, then:

'Why? What's this supposed to be about?'

'Oh, Sayers,' Gently said. 'We seem to have our hands on him.'

A longer silence!

Cockfield said: 'Just you – nobody else?'

'Just me,' Gently said.

Cockfield sounded as though he'd been drinking.

CHAPTER SIXTEEN

S PURS HAD WON 5–2, which was happiness enough
for Dutt. After tea he retired to the lounge to read
the print off a football special.

During tea Villiers had looked in, but seemingly
hadn't known what to say to them. He congratulated
them several times, but kept sheering away from
detailed comment.

'This is another success for you, Superintendent . . .
I'm glad our man showed up well in it.'

'Inspector Perkins showed great courage.'

'Yes . . . actually, we've just been talking . . .'

What he wanted to say was: Let it drop – get to hell
out of my manor! But apparently he couldn't hit on a
diplomatic way of phrasing it.

'You'll be glad of your leave after this . . .'

'Are you an angler by any chance?'

'No, not really . . . I do some fishing . . .'

In the end he gave up.

The sky had clouded over very lightly and the
evening was cooler. When Gently set out to

Weston-le-Willows the light had a filtered, shadowless radiance.

He drove, pipe in mouth, letting the Rover amble at forty. After Hawkshill, where he left the A-road, he met no traffic other than cyclists.

He arrived at Cockfield's chalet at seven. Three cars were already parked there. Along with the maroon Daimler and Hastings's Jaguar stood a spotless Volkswagen . . . Ashfield's, of course.

Gently parked the Rover beside it, slammed his door loudly, went up the steps.

Before he could ring, Cockfield opened to him.

Cockfield held a glass in his hand.

'Was there anyone else who ought to have been here?'

Surely it was quite an obvious question! Gently asked it casually while re-lighting his pipe, rather as a chairman might check his committee.

But nobody was rushing to give him an answer, Cockfield, Ashfield or Hastings. Instead they'd drawn together in a group and were eyeing Gently as though he would bite.

Cockfield had changed from his squire-like tweeds into a suit which suggested half-mourning. His moonish face had a droop in it, reminding Gently of Perkins.

Hastings, also holding a drink, had his mouth set sullenly; Ashfield stood with feet planted apart, a short, shiny-pated bulldog.

What did they think? That Gently had brought three warrants in his pocket?

'Come on . . . no need to be shy. We haven't been here fitting microphones. I could have hauled you down to Headquarters if I'd wanted to play games.

'What about Herbert Drinkstone?'

No reaction to Herbert Drinkstone!

'Or Joe Leyton? Or the ladies?'

Just three defensive stares . . .

'At least you can offer me a drink. I'll have a Scotch and soda.'

It was an appeal Cockfield couldn't resist and he went silently to the drinks cabinet. The other two, as though this were a signal, let their eyes slant away from Gently. Ashfield remained standing. Hastings chose a chair and sat.

Gently took the drink.

'Skaal!'

Cockfield made a token gesture.

Gently said: 'Perhaps it's time I brought you people up to date. Shimpling's dead. He was killed last night. We're holding Groton for the murder. Groton destroyed all Shimpling's material, nobody has anything to fear from that.

'Also, we've a statement from a Miss Banks, sometime known as Mrs Shimpling, in which she names all the people Shimpling was blackmailing in Abbotsham. But, of course, she's an unreliable witness and her testimony would need holstering.

'It's on the cards we wouldn't waste the ratepayers' money on that . . .'

He sipped the drink, looked at each of them.

'Any comment?' he inquired.

Hastings was gripping his glass tightly. He said: 'You wouldn't be kidding us . . . not about Shimpling?'

'No kidding. He was killed.'

'Then you know about Sammy?'

Gently nodded. 'Not to prove, of course. We couldn't offer evidence of identification. But between you, me and these four walls, it was Sammy the tiger ate — wasn't it?'

Hastings glanced at Cockfield, who grunted.

He said: 'Shimpling's dead, and you're holding Groton . . . ?'

'That's it.'

'For murdering Shimpling?'

'We're holding him on another charge, temporarily.'

'And he's made a statement?'

'No statement.'

'But he will make a statement!'

Gently shrugged. 'I don't think he will, and it'll only be relevant as it concerns the charge.

'Obviously, he may talk a lot of stuff about Shimpling and the tiger, and what he says will be passed on to the local police for action. But there again, proof is everything, and where is that proof to come from?

'I haven't found any yet, and I doubt whether Abbotsham will be luckier . . .'

They were all staring at him again, but now the stare was rather different!

Hastings said: 'Are you trying to tell us you intend to drop the case?'

Gently waved his glass. 'That's up to the locals. I'm

204

off on a fishing trip tomorrow. Naturally, I'll leave them certain advice about the conduct of the case.'

'Then what are you saying?' Cockfield burst out. 'Stop bloody well playing at cat-and-mouse with us. I've had enough – we all have. This isn't so damn funny, I can tell you.'

'What I advise them,' Gently said, 'rather depends on you gentlemen.'

'How on us?'

'I shall have to be satisfied about the facts of what happened.'

Cockfield glared at him. 'You mean a confession.'

'Confirmation, let's say.'

'You want us to incriminate ourselves.'

'It would be your three words against mine.'

'This is a trap!' Ashfield snapped. 'I warned you how it would be. He has his reputation to think of – he'll stop at nothing to put us inside.'

'I'm simply making you an offer,' Gently said. 'That's the Abbotsham way, isn't it? Give me the facts off the record, and perhaps you'll hear no more about this.'

'Perhaps, perhaps!' Ashfield scoffed. 'You've already admitted you've no proof.'

'I didn't admit I couldn't get proof . . .'

'Yes, after we've given ourselves away!'

'Hold it, Ken.'

Hastings laid his hand on Ashfield's arm.

'Letting him get your goat is dangerous – and there's a lot in what he says.'

'He thinks we're fools!'

'No he doesn't. He's right about saying we're three to one. If he tried to use anything we told him we could swear blind he was a liar.'

'But we might give him a lead—'

'How should we? Outside our testimony, where is there proof? He knows that, it's why he's here. And if it will stop him digging, I'm for telling him.'

'Let him dig.'

'I don't think he wants to.'

Cockfield said: 'I don't know if I trust him. But it's a fact he's come here alone. He can't use what we say as evidence.'

'Skaal!' Gently said. 'Drink up.'

Cockfield's glass twitched involuntarily.

'All right,' Ashfield said. 'Go ahead. But just remember I warned you when you're standing in the dock.'

Hastings gave him a wry smile. 'It's a place I've stood in before,' he said.

Now they were all sitting down, making a semicircle round the coffee table. Gently had Hastings on his left, between himself and Cockfield.

Through the window in front of them they could see the evening sunlight slanting on the lawn, the boathouse, and across the river, over the trees, hung red and ghostly the harvest moon.

Had there been moonlight a year ago, when three of these men had sat round this table? Had they noticed it, the colour of it, and found it dreadfully apposite?

But by the time the car left, the blood on the moon would have faded away . . .

'I'm going to tell this in my own way – I'll only identify Groton and Sammy.'

Hastings looked at Gently questioningly.

Gently nodded. 'That'll do.'

'There were five of us – six of us – being blackmailed by Shimpling. Who else he was biting we don't know. There were only five of us in the plot.

'At first we didn't know about each other, but then one of us, Groton, decided to hit back. He had it in mind to murder Shimpling and his plan required accomplices. He knew that Shimpling would have other victims. He hired a detective to run them down. He got on to Sayers and the three others and put up the tiger plot to them.'

Hastings hesitated awkwardly.

'Well, it was a good plot!' he said. 'We didn't like it, but it was a way out, and one of us was getting desperate.

'The objection made was about the woman, but just at that time she left Shimpling. So we agreed – two to do it, two to give them an alibi. Groton couldn't be in it, of course, he'd be the first person the police would check.

'Groton briefed us about the tiger and the way to release it from the truck. Sayers was one of the two who were to do it – he knew judo, he could tackle Shimpling. He wasn't keen, but he was the obvious choice . . . and he was the other man's friend.'

Gently said: 'You'd know him well, of course.'

Hastings jerked: 'None of that! What you guess is your affair, but I won't be cross-questioned.'

Gently shrugged. 'Sayers no doubt had a number of friends in Abbotsham . . .'

Hastings looked at him, was silent a moment. Then he went on flatly:

'We set it up for a night when Groton had a meeting in London. Sayers and the others were ostensibly spending a weekend in the country. At half past ten Sayers and the other man drove to Groton's farm to pick up the truck. Groton had left the tiger loaded in it and the doors of the body taken off.

'They drove it by back ways to Shimpling's bungalow. They arrived there at twenty past eleven. They stopped short of the bungalow and Sayers went ahead to reconnoitre. He opened the gates and signalled to the truck. The truck was driven on the verge, then backed to the gates. Sayers gave a thumbs-up sign to the driver, went up the drive, knocked, got set . . .'

Hastings screwed his eyes shut.

'Ted,' he said, 'fill my glass for me.'

Cockfield scrambled up, took the glass to the cabinet, brought it back full of whisky. Hastings drank.

He said: 'I wasn't watching. I was all tensed up with what I had to do. Sammy was fast, a black-belt man, he was going to chop him, get clear . . .

'When I saw the light showing I was to back in, raise the grille. I did that.'

He took a great throatful of whisky.

'God,' he said, 'it was fiendish! Groton had starved the bloody tiger. It was out in a flash, roaring and tearing.

'I could see it holding the bloke down and ripping away at his shoulder, blood spewing in all directions . . . then its head was raised, chewing.

'Oh God, the sound of that flesh being torn . . .

'And Sammy, he should have been back in the truck.

'Then I looked again, it was at his throat . . . the head came up.

'Sammy!'

Hastings sobbed, crammed the glass to his mouth.

'That's enough, Dave!' Cockfield cried. 'We can pick it up from there.'

'No.' Hastings shook his head. 'Let me finish.'

He sat holding the glass in both hands, holding it high, near his mouth.

'I deserve it,' he said. 'I bloody deserve it. I was the one who talked you over.

'But it was inhuman . . . terrible! When I think of it I want to scream. And I've seen some grim things . . . every doctor has his scars.

'What sort of a devil can Groton be? He knew. He knew!'

Hastings tipped the glass again.

'My nerve went,' he said. 'I had a blackout, something like that, I can't remember things till I got back here. I must have driven the truck to the farm, picked up my car, driven to Weston. But the next I remembered is being back here, trying to tell them, drinking.

'If anyone claims they've done things during a blackout, remember that. It can happen.'

He sat back, resting the now-empty glass against his chest. His eyes were slitted, as though seeing something they craved to shut out.

'He put the wind up us,' Cockfield said. 'Just to see him gave you a scare.'

Ashfield said: 'His hair was lifting – not on end: simply lifting.'

'I take it he didn't go back,' Gently said.

Cockfield said: 'Not so likely! We poured a bottle of Scotch into him and left him blotto on the sofa.'

'Then it was you two.'

Cockfield nodded.

'Did you . . . take a gun with you?'

'A four-ten. It's all I keep here. It wouldn't have made the brute sneeze.'

Gently said: 'It would have needed guts.'

Cockfield looked at him owlishly.

'When there's only one thing to do you bloody do it,' he said. 'That's all.'

'Tell me about it.'

'What for? You know what happened as well as I do.'

'Tell me about it,' Gently said.

Cockfield sat looking at him.

Ashfield said: 'You don't rattle me. We went to the bungalow and buried Sammy. It was bloody as hell, blood everywhere, soaking in blood, like a slaughterhouse. The bones were sticking out of his legs, half his face was eaten off . . .'

Ashfield stopped. He'd gone grey.

'I'm going to be sick,' he said weakly.

210

He got to his feet, stumbled out, and they could hear him retching in the toilet.

'Satisfied?' Cockfield said.

Gently hunched a shoulder. 'Was he sick that night?'

'You bloody swine,' Cockfield said. 'He was sick as a dog. And so was I.'

'Who carried the body to the wheelbarrow?'

'Me. He was outside with the gun.'

'What did you do about your clothes?'

'Burned them. Then we got as drunk as David.'

'Why didn't you go back and clean up properly?'

Cockfield shuddered. 'We always meant to. But we put it off, kept putting it off. I'll be sick too if you don't shut up.'

'What did you find when you searched the place?'

'Nothing. He must have taken it with him.'

Cockfield gulped, put a hand to his mouth. But he didn't follow Ashfield to the toilet. Hastings, looking at nobody, rose and went to fill his glass.

Outside, the moon was clear of the trees but was still a medallion of angry red.

Ashfield came back and drank some soda water, sat down, looked very unwell.

Hastings said through his teeth: 'Is that everything – have we done enough confessing?'

Gently drank a little, said: 'There's a matter of twenty thousand pounds . . .'

Cockfield said: 'Forget about it. Sammy left his money to Dave. Sammy didn't have any relatives. We've seen the will. It's pukka.'

'You've seen a will?'

Hastings said: 'There was a copy in Sammy's box. It was drawn by Dale and Perks. It's at the office. I can show it you.'

'But . . . it will hardly have gone for probate?'

'How the devil could it have done?'

'And you have the money?'

'We couldn't leave it there. The bank would have started investigations.'

Gently nodded. 'A problem, admittedly! And the Inland Revenue . . . what about them?'

'Look,' Hastings said, 'I haven't touched the money, and the Inland Revenue can stick itself.

'Sammy was concerned with famine relief, he used to make donations to Oxfam. At Christmas last year they collected a bonus – an anonymous twenty-one thousand pounds. Tax, death duties unpaid. And to hell with the whole bag of them!

'Are you a friend of the Inland Revenue?'

Gently shook his head. 'Not my department.'

'Well, that's where Sammy's money has gone.'

Gently stared at his glass, said nothing.

Cockfield said: 'So where do we stand now?'

Gently sighed, rose, held out his glass. He touched Hastings's, touched Cockfield's, made a token wave towards the chemist.

'What's this?' Cockfield demanded.

'A toast – to the guardian angel of Abbotsham.'

'To who?'

'Drink your whisky.'

Over his glass, Cockfield watched Gently suspiciously.

212

★ ★ ★

Dutt was still in the lounge when Gently returned to the Angel, but now he was watching a TV sportsflash of James Greaves getting a hat-trick. Perkins was with him. Perkins was showing no outward interest in James Greaves. He was sitting bolt upright in an easy chair and murmuring soundlessly, it may have been prayers.

When Gently approached he leaped up, but all he could blurt was:

'You've got back, then . . . !'

After which he stood pitifully, mouth gaping, eyes pleading.

Dutt, who'd also looked round, contented himself with a quick nod, then jerked his eyes back to the screen before he could miss half a pass.

Gently's pipe was going. He puffed affably. He glanced at the screen for a moment.

He said: 'One day you'll have to pull in friend Cockfield for drunken driving.'

'D-drunken driving?'

'I watched him this evening. He was all over the road.'

'But just . . . driving . . . ?'

'That's enough, isn't it? He's had one bad accident already.'

Really it was too bad! Perkins was almost wringing his hands. He jiffled and gaped and rolled his eyes, began a dozen sentences that never came out. Then he managed to stammer:

'And the inquest . . . Monday . . . ?'

'Put in evidence of how it was done.'

213

'That Sayers—'

'Not Sayers, you ass! Do you want to give the game away?'

'Then who – how . . . ?'

Gently closed his eyes. Did he have to teach them how to cover up? Here he was handing it to them on a plate, and still it didn't seem enough . . .

He drew Perkins aside.

'First, show the remains aren't Shimpling's! If you as much as whisper "Sayers" I'll come back here and strangle you personally. Then show that a crime was attempted against Shimpling by the deceased and persons unknown, and offer your opinion that the deceased met his death while committing that attempt. That's all. Nothing else! Let the coroner vapour about Groton if he wants to.

'Privately you can tell him you've no proved evidence of the identity of the deceased, and that offering an opinion on it might injure innocent people.

'Which it may – hard fact! Stick to that, and you're home.'

For a moment Perkins gaped glass-eyed at nothing. Then he swung round, grabbed Gently's hand and began to pump it with fervent violence.

'I can't tell you . . . we're all grateful . . . I . . .'

'Here . . . watch my hand!'

'. . . how much it means . . . us . . . Abbotsham . . .'

'Turn it up! People are looking.'

The damned idiot! For over a minute he was shaking away and blubbering thanks, while half the guests and Barnes, the pressman, were peering curiously in their direction.

'And if you're ever this way again . . .'

At last Gently managed to rescue his hand.

'Myself . . . my wife . . .'

'Put a cork in, will you? I missed my dinner, I'm blasted hungry.'

Dutt, his sportsflash ended, looked round perplexedly, and Barnes was beginning to sidle over.

But still that idiot burbled away, trembling with gratitude, almost weeping.

CHAPTER SEVENTEEN

GROTON CHARGED WITH
SHIMPLING MURDER
Bungalow Body Unidentified
Tiger: Attempt That Misfired

Hugh Groton, 52, an animal dealer from South Africa, was charged yesterday with the murder of Peter Shimpling.

But police failed to identify the tiger-victim at the resumed inquest at Abbotsham. They think now he was an accessory in a previous attempt on Shimpling.

Chief Superintendent Gently of the Yard, who has been assisting the local police, admitted to our reporter he thought identification unlikely . . .

A long way from Abbotsham, a long way from London. Two men sitting in a boat on a grey lake under slate mountains.

Superintendent Evans says: 'That's a bite, man! Why, you'll never catch a gwyniad.'

Gently shrugs, makes a strike, reels in an unbe-
lievable depth of line. The freshwater shrimp is gone
from his hook. He feels about the bait-can, finds a
replacement.

Evans says sternly: 'You must be more alert, man.
The gwyniad is a very delicate feeder. Catching the
gwyniad is a great art. Very few are the anglers who
catch a gwyniad.'

'Have you ever caught one?' Gently asks.

'No, I can't say I have,' Evans says. 'But I tell you, I
know what I'm talking about. And there are surely
gwyniad in Bala lake.'

Gently patiently rebaits his hook and lowers away
many fathoms. At the other end of the boat Evans sits
like a crouching griffin.

'That was a peculiar case of yours, man,' he says.
'What with tigers and leopards and that sort of animal.
I'm glad we haven't the like in Wales. No, not even
badgers we have.' A little silence, then Gently said:

'I don't believe that about the badgers.'

'No?' Evans says. 'Would you call me a liar – apart
from being Welsh, and a liar by nature?'

A little more silence, where all is silence.

A long way from Abbotsham, a long way from
London.

Two men sitting in a boat on a grey lake under slate
mountains.